"What's going on, Jack?"

"Nothing." Jack c[...]

"Don't think you c[...]
it. What's up?"

He couldn't revea[...]
about her.

That her admission about her feelings for him had started a chain reaction in him that made him feel he wasn't as content with his life as he had once thought. Not after all his denials and disagreement.

Instead, he shook his head. "It's nothing. Work stuff." He paused. "Are you interested in adopting a kitten? Bit of a fighter with other cats, but loves to snuggle with humans. He'd be great in a one-pet family. As a vet, I can highly recommend it."

"I told you, Jack. I'm not interested in having a pet." She touched the tip of his nose with her finger. "Even you can't change my mind about that."

"I'll wear you down eventually."

She laughed and he followed her outside the clinic...wondering what he was going to do with these new feelings that had arisen.

Dear Reader,

In this story, Melanie Beach is living my dream life. She owns a bookstore that is dedicated to bringing books to her community and nurturing a love for reading. I often daydream about quitting my day job and buying my own bookstore (with a coffee bar, of course). I'd host book clubs, writing critique groups and author book signings. To spend my working hours surrounded by books? Yes, please. Definitely my dream.

Melanie also lives my disappointments. I, too, have been relegated to friend status with a guy when I was more interested in being his girlfriend. I have to admit that this was a hard book to write because it hit very close to my own romantic life, and many of the dating disasters come directly from my own experience! I made sure that Melanie got the happy ending she deserved, but getting to that point brought lots of headaches and tears (for us both)—the sad and happy kind.

I hope you enjoy the story and the holidays!

Syndi

HEARTWARMING

A Merry Christmas Date

———

Syndi Powell

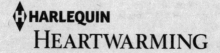

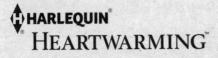

HARLEQUIN®
HEARTWARMING™

ISBN-13: 978-1-335-42653-6

A Merry Christmas Date

Copyright © 2021 by Cynthia Powell

Recycling programs
for this product may
not exist in your area.

This edition published by arrangement with Harlequin Books S.A.

For questions and comments about the quality of this book,
please contact us at CustomerService@Harlequin.com.

Harlequin Enterprises ULC
22 Adelaide St. West, 40th Floor
Toronto, Ontario M5H 4E3, Canada
www.Harlequin.com

Printed in U.S.A.

Syndi Powell started writing stories when she was young and has made it a lifelong pursuit. She's been reading Harlequin romance novels since she was in her teens and is thrilled to be on the Harlequin team. She loves to connect with readers on Twitter, @syndipowell, or on her Facebook author page, Facebook.com/syndipowellauthor.

Books by Syndi Powell

Harlequin Heartwarming

The Bad Boy's Redemption
A Hero for the Holidays
Soldier of Her Heart
Their Forever Home
Finding Her Family
Healing Hearts
Afraid to Lose Her
The Sweetheart Deal
Two-Part Harmony
Risk of Falling
The Reluctant Bachelor

Visit the Author Profile page
at Harlequin.com for more titles.

This book is dedicated to Kathryn Lye, my editor for eleven books here at Harlequin. Due to your commitment to excellence in storytelling, you have shaped and guided my stories to places that I didn't think possible. Thank you for your words of encouragement and advice.

CHAPTER ONE

MELANIE BEACH HAD loved only one man her entire life. The one problem was that he didn't seem to realize it.

From the passenger seat of a car on the way to the airport, she snuck a glance at Jack Cuthbert, her best friend and the object of her affections, as he turned onto the exit for drop-off and departures. He kept his gaze on the road, so she turned to find her other best friend, Shelby Cuthbert, making out with her boyfriend, Josh Riley, in the back seat. She cleared her throat, and the couple broke apart. "You'll have plenty of time for that on your trip."

Shelby gave a squeal and did a little dance in her seat, restrained only by the seat belt across her chest. "I can't believe this is really happening. We're actually heading to Greece. This is the dream trip I've been planning for years."

"How long do you intend on staying?" Jack asked from the driver's seat, glancing briefly into the rearview mirror at them.

Josh cupped Shelby's chin in his hand and kissed the tip of her nose before saying, "As long as my love wants to stay and explore the islands."

"But a minimum of two weeks." Shelby leaned in and rested her forehead against his. "I need at least that much time to see everything on my bucket list."

"You realize that a bucket list usually has a few items on it, not two pages of a detailed itinerary." Josh grinned.

Shelby gave him a playful shove. "You love my penchant for organizing every minute of my day. And yours."

He grinned more. "And mine. You're right."

"I'm just glad we were able to get this one planned so quickly."

Josh tapped her nose. "We didn't have a choice. With your family's Christmas fundraiser, your great-aunt's wedding and my inauguration on New Year's Day, this was the only time we could both go."

"I wouldn't want to go without you."

"Same here."

Mel smiled at the couple who had started to kiss again, then shifted to look at Jack, whose eyebrows had furrowed and whose mouth made a tight line across his face. She nudged his shoulder. "What's that face for?"

He gave a short shake of his head. "Nothing. We're almost to the airport."

Mel's smile faded as she wondered if Jack would ever gaze at her as adoringly as Josh did with Shelby. Would he ever love her as much as she loved him? Because for Melanie, there was only one man who would ever possess her heart, and it was the one who sat next to her, driving the car.

Jack pulled the car up to the curb next to the international flight terminal, and the next few minutes were filled with retrieving suitcases from the trunk and passports from carry-on bags. Shelby and Josh checked in with the concierge at the luggage stand, then turned to Jack and Mel, Shelby's eyes growing damp as she pulled Mel into a tight hug. "I've never been this far away from you before. What am I going to do without you?"

Mel rubbed her back and snuck a glance at Josh who shook hands with Jack. "I think Josh will keep you guys too busy to miss me. Besides, we'll have texts and emails to keep in touch."

Shelby took a step back, then hugged Jack. Mel gave Josh a quick embrace. "Take care of Shelby. She's like a sister to me."

"Don't worry. I'm going to guarantee that this is the trip of a lifetime for her."

Mel liked the man Josh had become. She could well remember the bad boy that he had been in high school. How he'd broken Shelby's heart, then moved away only to win her back twelve years later when he returned to their suburban Michigan town of Thora. He had truly changed into a good man that was worthy of her best friend. "You better."

Shelby put her hand in Josh's and waved with the other. "I guess this is it. Thanks again for the ride."

Jack thrust his hands into his pockets. "Anytime."

Shelby glanced at Mel, then they were hugging again, this time letting their tears fall unchecked down their cheeks. "I'll be back soon."

"I know, but I'm going to miss you every day until you return."

Shelby held her at arm's length. "I think it's time you tell him how you feel."

Mel snuck a peek at Jack, then shook her head. "No, it's not."

"What's the worst that could happen?"

Mel had asked herself the same question for years, and she always came back to the same answer. "It will be awkward if I tell him, and then I'll lose my best friend because he will never love me like that. But I recently ordered a book that talks about how to break out of the friend zone, and I think if I read it and apply everything the author—"

"Mel, when are you going to stop living through books and actually live your life?"

Mel shook her head. "You don't understand. This book is written by a psychiatrist who was in a similar situation and actually married her best friend. This is going to work. I know it will."

"I hope so, but I'm worried that you'll

let your chance with him slip through your fingers."

"No, I can't tell him. Not yet."

Shelby hugged her once more. "Promise me you'll think about it."

Mel nodded and let her friend go. Josh took Shelby's hand once more, and they entered the terminal, Shelby glancing behind her at them every few feet. Once they were out of view, Mel noticed Jack's frown had returned. "Why have you been so cranky this morning?"

"I don't know what you're talking about." He glanced behind them at his car still parked at the curb. "We should go before I get a ticket or my car gets towed."

Mel followed him back to the curb and got into the car. She put on her seat belt, then tried to study him. "Ever since Shelby announced she was going to Greece with Josh, you've been in a bad mood. What is going on?"

"It's nothing."

"Why can't you be happy for Shelby? She's finally going after something she wants, and that includes Josh."

Jack didn't answer for a moment as he

pulled away from the curb and merged with traffic heading back to the highway. "I know that Josh won you and the entire town over, but I don't trust him. I don't want my cousin to end up with a broken heart."

"She loves him, and he loves her just as much."

"Love isn't always enough."

Now Mel was frowning. She knew he was right about that. Her loving Jack might not be enough. She faced forward. Which is why she wouldn't tell him. Maybe not ever.

MEL CONTINUED TO peruse the menu as the waitress placed their mugs of coffee on the table. She then waited with her order pad in hand. Mel shook her head. "I'm sorry. I need another minute."

Jack sighed, knowing that she was stalling because she couldn't decide. "Just order the blueberry pancakes with bacon. That's what you always get."

"Just because you order the same thing every time doesn't mean that I have to."

Jack didn't know what was so wrong

with having his favorites and sticking to them. So what if he didn't want to try the latest and greatest? He knew what he liked and there was nothing wrong with that.

The waitress shot him a look. "I'll be right back."

He watched her leave, then turned to find Mel watching him. "Isn't she a little young for you?"

He held up his hands. "What? I'm not interested in the waitress."

She gave him a look that seemed to say she didn't believe a word he was saying. "You were looking at her."

And what is wrong with that? "I was. I just choose not to do anything beyond that right now."

Mel closed the menu and placed it next to her coffee cup. "And why aren't you dating? I figured that once your cousins started pairing off that you would be next."

Jack considered this as he took a sip of his coffee. First it had been Penny who had recently married the man who bought their great-aunt's house when his burned down. Now it was Shelby who had lost the election for mayor but won the heart of her opponent. When Jack placed the mug on the table, he gave a half-hearted shrug. "Right now is not a good time for me to pursue anything with anyone."

"Why? Because you struck out with the As?"

He smiled at the nickname that Mel had dubbed the last three women he dated: Angelique, Ashley and Amanda. "You should stop calling them that."

"Maybe it's time you moved to a different letter of the alphabet. Maybe somewhere in the middle?"

She looked up at the waitress who approached their table and asked, "Made a decision?"

Jack ordered his standard eggs over easy and crispy bacon as Mel studied the menu, then ordered her usual blueberry pancakes with a side of bacon. He tried not to gloat, but knew that he had failed when Mel frowned at him. "Don't give me that look. I couldn't decide on anything else."

"Because there's nothing wrong with liking what you always get."

"Maybe one day, I'll surprise you and order something different." She pulled her coffee cup closer and added cream, then sugar. "So back to you dating."

"Nothing to get back to because I told you that I'm not dating." He'd learned his lesson, and it wasn't one that he wanted to repeat. "I'm focusing on me and my career right now. I told you that I hired another vet for the clinic, right?"

He'd been burning the candle at both ends for years trying to get the animal clinic up and running. He'd lost his marriage and several relationships in the process, but his practice had gotten so busy that he had needed to hire another veterinarian. He only hoped that Lucas would stick and be able to take some of the burden off his shoulders.

"And it's about time too. You've been working too hard for too long."

"And that should be changing now with Lucas on staff. I won't be on call twenty-four seven anymore." Mel shot him a look that told him she didn't believe him. He shrugged. "But it's still my clinic. My baby. I'm the one responsible for it."

"You've always been very responsible. It's one of the things I love about you." She smiled across the table at him, and he returned the grin.

"Back at you."

"Speaking of our businesses, are you coming to my Halloween party a week from Sunday?"

Jack groaned. "You're never open on Sundays. Why do I have to go?"

"It's Halloween, so it's special. I always have a Halloween party for the kids at the store. I'm not going to change that just because it falls on a Sunday."

"Of course I'll be there. I'll just have to leave Sunday dinner at my parents' house early." He scowled at the thought of Halloween. "I don't have to dress up, do I?"

"Costumes are encouraged, but not required."

He gave a sigh of relief. He knew that Mel was a big fan of Halloween, but it had never been one of his favorites. Dressing up. Pretending to be someone else. Begging for treats from strangers. He gave a shudder. He'd pass, thank you. "I'll wear my scrubs and be a veterinarian."

Mel sighed and shook her head. "You're never going to change, are you?"

"You probably wouldn't like me if I did."

She stared at him for a long moment, opening and shutting her mouth until she finally gave a soft shake of her head and added more sugar to her coffee.

"What was that about?"

"I needed more sugar."

"No, what were you thinking about just then?" She had looked as if she had wanted to say something, but had changed her mind at the last minute. "What's going on?"

Her cheeks colored, and she waved her free hand in the air between them. "It's nothing. Just…thinking about all I have to get ready for Halloween. Would you mind picking up a few more bags of candy before you stop by on Sunday? I don't think I have enough."

"Whatever you need, Mel. You know you can count on me."

PINT-SIZED SUPERHEROES, princesses and monsters raced around the bookstore before landing in front of the rocking chair in the children's section where Melanie waited with the evening's Halloween story. Dressed as a witch in a long black dress with a matching pointed black hat, she looked out into the bright, shiny faces of her audience. She opened the book and scanned their faces once more before starting to tell the story of Harold, the Reluctant Halloween Monster.

Halloween was one of her favorite times of the year. She could dress up and pretend to be someone else who was braver than she. Not that her life wasn't one that she was proud of. After all, she owned the bookstore which was a dream she'd had since being not much older than the children sitting on the carpet in front of her. She had two best friends who she would do anything for and they'd do the same for her. She had a cute little house that she'd renovated and decorated on her own by using books that she studied—applying the techniques within them. No, her life had a lot of good things.

It was missing only two that she wanted more than anything else—a husband and a family.

She paused in telling the story to look out at the audience again and found Jack leaning on a bookshelf, watching her performance. He gave her a smile and a wink.

If only she could believe that the wink meant something more.

Once the story had been told and the children returned to their parents, Melanie replaced the book on the shelf, then returned to the front of the store to help out her only other staff member, Emma, with ringing up sales and making hot drinks.

"Great performance as always," Jack said, lifting his mug of coffee in salute. He sat on a stool at the long wooden coffee bar, a new book next to him. She'd ordered that thriller last week especially for him since she knew his preferences as well as her own when it came to reading.

"Thank you as always." She held out the hem of her black skirt and gave a quick curtsy.

He glanced around the store, and she wondered what he saw. The store was one large room with wooden paneling and hardwood floors; except in the children's section which was carpeted with squares in primary colors. Bookshelves created a maze for a reader to get lost in while searching for the next great book. Maybe she had gone overboard with the Halloween decorations this year, but she couldn't help it. And the kids loved all the pictures of their favorite characters dressed in costumes. "I've never understood why this was your favorite holiday." He turned back to her. "I mean, I get it when you're a kid and it's all about the candy. But you're an adult now."

"Halloween isn't just about candy. It's about getting the chance to be someone else for one night."

He peered at her. "And who would you want to be besides yourself?"

Your date. She hoped he couldn't detect the longing in her eyes as she looked at him. To change the subject, she pointed to his coffee mug. "Need a refill?"

"If I have any more, I won't be able to sleep tonight." He patted the book next to him. "Although this might do it as well. I can't wait to dive into the story."

"You might need some caffeine if you're going to help me put the store back to rights after everyone leaves. Emma has to get to a Halloween party, so I told her she could leave early."

Jack groaned, but did so with a smile. "Why do you always rope me into these things?"

"You're an easy mark. And Shelby would help me too if she wasn't halfway around the world with Josh."

"Have you heard from her recently?"

They'd had a brief phone call that had left Mel longing to do some traveling herself. "She called last night. They're staying at a hotel on a beach in Milos." Melanie sighed and rested her chin on her fist. "From everything she says, it's so romantic. We should go sometime."

"Think I'll leave the world traveling to you and my cousin." Jack pushed off the stool and grabbed the book. "After you close the store, come find me in an armchair. I'll be in the mystery section. Think I'll read a few pages while I wait."

He left, and Melanie watched his progress. Did he know how much she cared about him? Couldn't he see how much she wanted to take a romantic vacation with him? Or even go on a real date for just once with him? Sure, they went out to dinner at least once a week, but Jack kept everything strictly in the friend zone. Mel was still hopeful that reading her latest book would help her get past that label.

A vampire dressed in scrubs approached her. One of the few adults who had dressed for the holiday, Mel stifled a giggle at his appearance. "Are you Dr. Dracula?"

The vampire pulled the edge of his scrubs top out. "I want to take your blood, then send it to the lab for tests," he said, then shrugged. "I work as a nurse at the hospital, and my patients are always calling me a vampire, so I followed their suggestion for Halloween this year."

"Clever."

"That I am." He pointed behind him at the children's section. "Could I get your opinion about something? I need to pick out a book for my nephew's birthday and have no clue what would be appropriate."

"How old is he?"

"Eight going on eighty."

She followed him into the rows of books, pulling a couple off the shelves as they walked. "If he's into sports, I'd recommend these two."

"No sports. He loves his video games instead."

"Gotcha." She replaced the two and grabbed another. "This is the first book of a new series that he might enjoy, full of wizards, magic and dragons. Very popular right now. Word is that the author is in talks with producers to turn her series into a movie."

"They write books before the movie is made?"

She put a hand on her chest. "You have to read the book before seeing it. It's practically the law in my world."

He smiled. "I'd be interested in getting a glimpse of your world. Or maybe just take you to a movie some night." He held out his hand. "I'm Marius."

She shook hands with him. "Melanie, but my friends call me Mel." Was he asking her out? To avoid answering, she let go of his hand and grabbed another couple of books from a nearby shelf. "Eight-year-old boys also like the gross humor in these."

"I'll take them all. And maybe your phone number?"

He gave her a bright smile, and Mel tried to feel something like she did for Jack. But nothing. Maybe a mild interest in his life story, but otherwise she wasn't attracted to him. Even if he was a tall, good-looking man with short dark hair and chocolate-brown eyes that twinkled with a sense of humor that she liked. Okay, so she was attracted, but not enough to act on it. She shook her head. "I don't think that's a good idea, Marius."

"You're not wearing a ring, so it must mean you've given your heart to someone else." He gave a loud, exaggerated sigh. "Guess I'll have to become a regular customer here and win you over to my side with time. I am a man with patience." He tugged on the neckline of his scrubs. "Patients? Get it?"

She couldn't help but return his smile as he gave her a quick nod, then left her in the children's section while she wondered why she couldn't get over her crush on Jack.

Once everyone, including Emma, had left for the evening, Jack placed the last few dirty dishes into the small dishwasher under the coffee counter as she balanced the cash register and placed the drawer in the safe below for safekeeping overnight. Mel turned off the lights and gathered the zippered pouch that held the deposit to be dropped off at the bank in the morning on her way in to work and placed it in her purse. Jack waited for her at the front door. "Another successful night for Mel's Books. I saw a lot of kids leaving with new books to read, and a number of parents with their own picks."

"It's my duty to encourage a love of reading in the children and adults of Thora. And if I can do it with candy and costumes, all the better."

Jack started to open the door, but Melanie stayed his hand. "Before we leave, could we talk for a minute?"

"Now? In the dark?"

"If I turn the lights back on, I might lose my courage." She swallowed at the fear that made her feel as if her body had become fragile. Breakable. She knew that she should wait to tell Jack about her feelings, but there was something in the air tonight.

The festivities of the Halloween party had given her a sense of bravery to do something. To tell him the truth finally and face the consequences of it afterward, whatever those might be. Or maybe it was the interest from another man who didn't see her as the safe best friend. She should tell him.

The more she waited to say something, she wondered if letting it go a little longer would be better. Maybe give Jack more time to see that he might have feelings for her too. But Jo, the heroine of her favorite book, *Little Women*, wouldn't back down from speaking her mind, and neither would she.

She placed her hand on Jack's, and he grasped it, his eyes searching her face. "What is it? You're scaring me a little."

The light from the street lamp outside her store lit up the hard planes of his handsome face, and she was drawn as she always was to his bright blue eyes, a Cuthbert family trait. Would he see her as the woman she was and not the friend he'd always known? She squeezed his hand. "The thing is, Jack, that I love you."

He smiled and put his free hand on her

shoulder. "I love you too, Mel. You know that. You're my best friend in the entire world."

She shook her head and closed her eyes. "I'm not talking as friends. I've been in love with you since I was six and you stood up to Kissing Kevin on my behalf on the playground at school." She opened her eyes to find Jack frowning, confusion creating shadows on his face. "I want to be more than your friend."

Jack let go of her hand and took a step back. "Mel…"

She frowned. "I've practiced this moment in my head for years, but now that it's here I'm getting the words all wrong."

"And I know how you love your words, but I think it's been a long day and we're both tired. That's all this is. We can laugh about this tomorrow."

"This isn't a joke." She reached up and held his face in her hands. "I'm offering you everything I have. All you have to do is say yes."

Jack closed his eyes. "I—"

"Friendship is the basis of a great relationship. We'll just be taking what we have to the next level." Before she could lose her nerve, she reached up and pressed her mouth to his.

In her fantasies, this moment had been so much more. The kiss would awaken him to what had been in front of him all this time. He would truly see her and want her like she wanted him to.

But him pushing her away had never happened in those dreams.

CHAPTER TWO

JACK STEPPED AWAY from Mel and put a finger against his lips that had just been touching Mel's. Had she really kissed him? Why was she doing this? Jack wanted to rewind these last few minutes and stop her from telling him anything. To keep her from changing the relationship they had. Because in his mind, it was perfect as it was. It didn't need more than what they had.

He'd meant what he said when he said he loved her too, but not like this. She was the one woman in his life who would never leave him. He depended on her to always be there.

"Kiss me again and tell me what you feel," she said and leaned toward him again.

"Stop it, Mel." The words came out sharper than he intended. When she dropped her hand from his shoulder and started to step away, he reached for her hand to keep her from running away like he knew she wanted to. "Why are you trying to change what we have? Isn't it enough for you?"

"No, that's the point I'm trying to make here. This is not nearly enough for me." She bit her lip, shaking her head. "I want a home with you. And children, if you want that." She dropped her gaze to the wood floor. "And sex. Haven't you ever wondered about what that would be like between us?"

Jack thought about sex, sure, but he hadn't thought of her in that way since they'd been in their teen years. Instead, his relationship with her was safe, predictable and comfortable, but not sexy. Mel was his soft place to fall when life dropped him. His support when he lost a patient. She wasn't his object of lust. They didn't have those kinds of fireworks between them. And they never would.

He turned away from her because he couldn't bear to see the pain in her eyes.

"Why are you doing this? You're ruining what we already have."

"But what if it only made it better?" She walked up behind him, and he felt her hand on his shoulder, but he flinched away from her touch. When her voice came, it was low, almost strangled. "I love you, Jack. And I'm not getting any younger."

He turned back around and searched her face to see if he could figure out why she felt this need to change everything between them. "Is that where this is coming from? Your biological clock is going off?"

"It's more than that. I can't walk around with these feelings for you anymore and wonder if you feel the same." She looked into his eyes, and he felt as if she saw to his very core. "Don't you think you could ever be in love with me?"

Jack wanted to groan. Talk about being put on the spot. He'd rather avoid this entire conversation for the rest of his life. Avoid hurting her. But he stood and faced her, shaking his head. "No, I don't."

Mel stepped back as if he'd insulted her. "Oh. I see."

"I wish you hadn't said anything. I'm sorry, I never wanted to hurt you."

"But I was already hurting. Every time we're together, I ache from not being closer to you. With you. Obviously, it was one-sided, but I had hope that you would one day return my affections." She slid her purse strap higher onto her shoulder. "Now I see that I was wrong."

Jack could see the tears forming in her eyes, and he longed to wipe them away. To shield her from this pain. Because he knew in his heart that he couldn't be the man she needed. Sure, he was good at friendship but history had proven that he was a disaster at relationships. And Mel knew that more than anyone, since she had been there to help him pick up the pieces after his divorce. "I wish I could be who you need, but I'm not that man, Mel. I don't think I ever could be."

She closed her eyes, and a lone tear slid down her cheek. He watched as she took several deep breaths before looking at him and squaring her shoulders. In that moment, she reminded him of a warrior girding herself with armor and taking up her shield. "Then I think it's best if we take a break from each other."

He was surprised at her words. Being apart from her was not an option he'd ever thought of. "Because I don't love you means that I can't even be your friend now? You can't mean that."

"I think I need some space from you. You can't give me what I want, which I accept, but being around you only hurts because of that."

Jack was filled with fear that he was going to lose her anyway no matter what he said. "Mel, please don't do this. Don't end what we already have. You're my best friend, and I can't do this life without you next to me."

She swiped another tear away and took several steps back. "But I want more than friendship. And if you can't give me that, then I need time and space to heal my heart. I need to move on from these feelings for you. Otherwise, this will always be between us, and our friendship will be doomed forever." She opened the door to her bookstore and waved her arm. "Please leave."

He couldn't let it end like this. Couldn't walk away from almost twenty-five years of friendship. "There has to be another way we can resolve this. Tell me what I can do to fix it, and I will."

"I can't make you love me, so what's the point?" She dropped her gaze to the floor. "Please, Jack." Her words came out soft, whispered but heavy with pain. "Just leave me."

He took one more look at her, then turned and walked out the door. He could hear her sobs even as she closed the door to the bookstore and locked it behind him.

AFTER CRYING HER sorrows out in the bookstore, then shedding more tears on her drive home, Mel let herself into her house. She hung her keys and purse on the hooks near the front door. She closed her eyes and wished she hadn't said a word to Jack. Why hadn't she just kept things as they had been? Kept her feelings for him to herself like she had always done?

Because she was tired of being in love with Jack and not knowing if he could feel the same way.

Well, she certainly had her answer now.

Groaning, she dragged herself through the living room and down the hall to her bedroom where she flopped onto her bed. Without taking her clothes or shoes off, she pulled the comforter around her, burrowing into its fluffy softness.

She wanted to cry some more. To let it all out. But her body hurt all over, pushing any thoughts of tears to the side. She rolled onto her back and stared at the ceiling. Was her life always going to be like this? Coming home to an empty house with the only sounds her own breathing? Maybe she should act on Jack's constant suggestion that she get a pet. Hadn't he been after her to adopt one of the many strays that he had found over the years?

Needing to talk to someone, she got out of bed and searched for her cell phone. She found it in her coat pocket by the front door and dialed Shelby's number. She would call her other best friend because calling Jack was out of the question.

The phone rang five times, and Mel realized that it was probably close to four in the morning in Greece. She was about to hang up, but Shelby picked up on her end and whispered, "Mel?"

"Shel, I didn't realize the time difference. Sorry. Go back to sleep."

"It's okay. You wouldn't have called unless it was important. Just give me a moment to step outside." Mel waited until Shelby returned on the line, still whispering. "Okay, I can talk now."

"Where are you?"

"On the balcony of our hotel room. I came out here so I wouldn't wake up Josh."

Something was going on with Shelby. Mel could sense it. It was more than sharing a hotel room with Josh, but she couldn't put her finger on the difference. Something in her voice seemed to indicate a change in her. She paused. "This is going to seem weird, but you sound different somehow."

"Do I? I guess I am. I have to tell you something, but you have to promise to not tell anyone. Not even Jack."

"I promise."

"Not. Even. Jack."

She winced at the words. "You don't need to worry about that. We're not talking right now."

"What happened this time? Is that why you called?"

"It doesn't matter, Shel. What's your news?"

Shelby took a deep breath on the other end. "We got married last night."

Melanie stopped walking down the hallway to her bedroom, her mouth hanging open, trying to understand what Shelby was telling her. Married? How? "You did what?"

"Josh and I got married." Shelby chuckled on the other end. "We were walking hand in hand on this beach when we saw this couple getting married there, and I thought to myself that it must be so romantic, and how I wished it was us. Well, I guess I must have said it aloud because Josh said, 'Then let's do it.' So we found a priest, who could fast-track the official paperwork, and we did it."

"I can't believe you got married." And that Mel hadn't been there to witness it. When they had been nine, she and Shelby had made a pact to be each other's maid of honor when the time came. A small sense of betrayal warred with the joy she felt for her friend, but the delight for her friend won out. "Wow. Congratulations! That's amazing news."

"But you can't tell anyone. I don't want to even think what my family might say if they find out about what we did without them here to be a part of it. We'll have to figure out how to tell them once we get home."

"I'm so happy for you." And she meant it. She knew that Shelby and Josh would be good for each other. "We'll have to have a big party when you get back. A wedding reception where you can renew your vows for everyone to see."

"I was going to call and tell you in the morning, but you called me first." Shelby paused, then asked, "So, now your turn, Mel. What's wrong?"

"It doesn't matter. We can talk about it when you get back home."

Shelby was quiet a moment. "No. You needed me. What's happened?"

"Oh, Shel, I really messed up." The tears that had stopped now flowed down her cheeks. "I'm afraid that I've lost Jack forever."

"You can do a lot of things to mess up, but you will never lose Jack, and you know it."

"You don't understand. I finally told him how I felt about him, and it was completely awful." Mel told her the whole story, rushing her words to get them out as quickly as she could. "He's so angry at me."

"I don't think it's anger. I think he's afraid of what this will mean for your friendship. And I know that the two of you will work this out."

"I don't think so. At least not anytime soon." She got off her bed and retrieved a couple tissues from the box on her dresser. "I've ruined everything. We can't go back to being friends after this."

"You don't know that."

"What I don't know is if I can be just his friend anymore. It was okay before because he didn't know I was in love with him, but now he does and I don't want to be just his friend." Mel blew her nose and wadded up the tissue. "I'm so tired of being alone. I want to be in a relationship and more someday. Why is that so wrong?"

"There's nothing wrong with wanting

that. Maybe Jack just needs some time to figure this out for himself."

"Do you think he'll ever love me?"

Shelby stayed quiet on the other end of the phone for a long time. "I don't know, Mel. But what I do know is that you two have a solid friendship that has withstood a lot over the years and neither one of you wants to let that go."

She tossed the used tissue on her nightstand next to the stack of books there. "I'm sorry. I don't mean to take away from your big news with my sad story."

"You haven't taken anything. I just wish I was there to hug you and tell you it's all going to be okay."

"I wish you were here too." She grabbed another tissue and dabbed it in the corners of her eyes. "Do you really think it's going to be okay?"

"Of course it is. You're an incredible woman who has so much to offer to anyone, and if Jack doesn't want that or can't see it, then maybe this was a sign that it's finally time to move on from these feelings for him."

"I did get asked out by this cute guy tonight at the bookstore, but I completely dismissed him because he wasn't Jack." Mel took a deep breath. "You're right. I have to move on."

"So what are you going to do next?"

"I'm going to stop crying and say yes to the next man who asks me out." Mel stood and walked to her closet and slid the door aside to peer inside at its contents. The blouses and pants looked drab in colors of gray, beige and navy with very few pops of color mixed in with them. When had she become so dowdy? It was past time to make a change. "I'm going to get a make-over and buy cute clothes and remind myself that there are other men besides Jack Cuthbert out there in the world. I swear to you that this is the last holiday I intend to spend alone."

JACK OPENED THE door to the animal clinic and walked inside. Whenever he was troubled, he sought refuge with the animals he treated and loved as if they were his own pets. And tonight, he was more than troubled. He worried that Mel's declaration to him had altered their friendship forever.

He turned lights on as he walked down the hall to where he kept the patients that stayed overnight. When he opened the door, the vet tech on duty looked up from the laptop in front of her and smiled. "Hey, Jack. I didn't know you were on call tonight."

"Hey, Alison. I was in the area and thought I'd stop in to see how things were going."

Two dogs greeted him with yips from their cages and a ferret crouched on his hind legs to see. Since he was there, he asked, "Hey, guys. Who needs to go outside for a bit?"

"I can do that. That's why you pay me the big bucks."

He waved away her offer. "I've got this. I could use some time with them."

She peered at him. "Dating troubles?"

If only she knew. He let the first dog out of his cage and put him on a leash. As he exited the back door, the golden retriever propelled him forward. "Guess it's a good thing I stopped in tonight when I did," he told the dog.

The golden retriever, who had been

named PJ by his three-year-old owner, stared at Jack until he held up a hand. "Fine. I'll give you some privacy."

He turned his back to the dog and stared up at the night sky. What he wouldn't give to have a shooting star to wish upon at that moment. He'd use that wish to go back to earlier that night and stop Melanie from having that conversation with him. What had she been thinking? Their friendship was the kind that most people would fight to have. So why would she take a risk and mess it up now?

Once both dogs had been taken outside, Jack topped up their food and water along with the ferret's before checking on the family of kittens he had rooming in a special space set up just for them. He scooped up a gray kitten that he had nicknamed Trouble and gently rubbed between his ears. "The sooner I get you adopted, the better. You need a child who will match your energy and curiosity."

He sat on the floor. Three other kittens approached him and started to climb onto his lap and up his arms as if he was their personal jungle gym. "I've missed you too," he told them, taking turns to give each a head scratch.

A yip from the other side of the room made him turn his head. "You'll all get your turn. Just wait."

Once the kittens had been loved on, he cleaned up their space before going and giving belly rubs to the puppies. He spied one of them watching him from behind the food dish. He'd been having difficulty socializing this puppy who he suspected had been neglected or abused before showing up outside the clinic tied to a light post. She had been skin and bones, shivering despite the warm September day. It had been six weeks, and she was no closer to letting him pet her than she had been on the first day.

He started to get onto his knees to crawl closer to her when his phone started barking. The puppies answered with their own yips, and he smiled as he answered the phone. "Dr. Cuthbert."

"It's Shelby."

He frowned and tried to figure out the time difference between them. "Shouldn't you be sleeping right now?"

"I was, but I just got a phone call that woke me up."

Jack sighed and sat back on his haunches. "Let me guess. Mel?"

"How could you do that to her, Jack?"

"Me? I'm not the one who tried to ruin almost twenty-five years of friendship."

He could almost see his cousin shaking her head at him. "She loves you. How is that ruining anything? Don't you think it would make your relationship with her even better?"

"Shel, you know my track record with women. I'm batting a big fat zero on that front." He stood and started to pace inside the puppy pen. "Besides, this is Mel we're talking about."

"And what's so wrong with that? Don't you love her?"

"Sure, I do. I always will."

"But…"

He sighed and ran a hand over his jaw where he'd started to grow out a beard. "But I don't think of her in that way."

"And why not? Melanie is a beautiful woman, inside and out. Any man would be lucky to have her love."

"I agree. He would be. But I'm not that man."

"How do you know? Have you even considered it?"

There had been a time the summer after they graduated high school when he had considered what dating Mel would be like, but that fall they had gone away to different colleges and the moment had passed. When they'd both moved back to Thora to pursue their careers, it seemed to be too late. Besides, he'd been head over heels for Stacey then and had soon after married her.

"It doesn't matter. I can't be the man she needs."

"You don't know that."

"Like I said before, I'm hopeless when it comes to women. The last thing I'd ever want to do is to lose Mel. She's my best friend, and I can't imagine living my life without her." He paused. "Is she really upset?"

"What do you think?"

He closed his eyes, grimacing at the thought that he'd made Mel cry. It hadn't been his intention to do that, but there was no way to get out of that awkward conversation without one of them being hurt. He regretted that it had been Mel who was in pain. He'd gladly take it upon himself and spare her if he could. "I'll call her tomorrow and make amends."

"If she takes your call. She's really upset with you."

"Is it that bad?" When Shelby didn't answer, Jack groaned. He'd known the answer to that question before he'd even asked, but he'd been hoping he was wrong. "I don't understand what was wrong with our friendship. It's been so important to me and I thought to her, as well."

"Because she wasn't happy with how things were, Jack. You need to fix this."

"I will." When his cousin didn't say anything else in reply, he sighed. "I promise. I'll make it up to her somehow. But getting involved in a romance with Mel will never happen."

CHAPTER THREE

AT THE END of a long day with heavy sales numbers, Mel locked up the bookstore and paused a moment before placing the key in her pocket. It had been two days since her declaration to Jack. He'd texted and called, but she needed a little more time, a little more space, before she could jump back into her friendship with him. She knew she would eventually because life without Jack didn't make sense.

She took her time walking down Main Street toward the parking lot where her car waited for her. The candle shop next door to hers had transformed their front window into a spectacular holiday display with white twinkle lights wound around red, green and ivory candle pillars. The sporting goods store had changed their mannequins from hiking apparel to skiing. And even the small grocery on the corner advertised specials on ham, fruitcake and baking supplies. One of the reasons she loved the location of her bookstore was the proximity to the other downtown Thora businesses. While she might have liked a closer parking spot, it would have meant less of a chance to do some fun window shopping from time to time.

And the newly formed Thora small business cooperative gave her an opportunity to draw on resources in the community to help her store. Shelby might not have won the election for mayor, but her ideas for helping businesses had sparked a positive transformation. Thora's businesses would have a hand in revitalizing the sleepy Detroit suburb and bringing in much-coveted jobs and tourist dollars.

Thinking about the co-op's next meeting, after the New Year, Mel almost missed the sight of the dog crouching under the rear of her car. She paused her steps and looked around to try and locate its owner. She walked closer to her car, and the dog stared at her. Remembering Jack's words about approaching a dog you didn't know with caution, she held her hands out, palms up. "It's okay. I'm not going to hurt you."

The dog continued to watch her approach. When she reached her car, she unlocked it and placed her purse inside with the intent of going back to check on the dog. But he must have had other ideas because when she turned, he had come up behind her and jumped past her to leap into the car. She stared at him as he sat in the driver's seat. "What do you think you're doing, mister? This is my car."

He stepped carefully over the center gear shift and settled into the passenger seat, then turned to look at her as if to say, "Okay, I'm in. Let's go."

"I'm not taking you anywhere. I don't know who you belong to," she told him. She went around the car to the passenger door and opened it, waving her arm toward the pavement. "Come on. Out of there."

He wagged his tail but stayed in the seat. Melanie looked at his neck and noticed he wasn't wearing a collar or any tags. She glanced around the parking lot again. This had to be a practical joke, right? Someone was setting her up by sending this dog to get in her car and refuse to leave. She narrowed her eyes at him. "Did Jack put you up to this?"

The dog started panting, looking almost as if he was smiling. She reached her hand out to him, and he sniffed it before allowing her to pet him. "Who do you belong to?"

His ribs showed under his fur, so she knew it had been a while since the dog had eaten. "Is someone looking for you, buddy?"

She rubbed under his chin, which seemed to produce an even wider smile and she decided she knew the perfect person to answer her question.

JACK MADE NOTES on the computer about his last patient, a ginger Maine coon cat who had started showing signs of feline leukemia. He wished he was wrong, but he'd seen the circumstances enough to know what to expect next. He only hoped that he could keep the cat as comfortable as possible while he explained his prognosis to his owner, Mr. Dadson. He'd know soon enough once the lab results were in.

A knock on the office door caught his attention. Starr, one of the vet techs, was standing there. "Do you have time for a walk-in? She says she knows you."

He glanced at his watch but knew the gesture was meaningless. Of course he would see whoever she was. "Put her in room two."

Starr nodded and left. Jack saved the file after making a final note to check on the status of the lab tests in the morning. He expected one of his cousins to be behind the exam room door, but finding Mel with a large dog sitting atop the table surprised him. "Mel, what are you doing here?"

She gestured to the dog. "I found him by my car and figured you'd know who he might belong to."

Jack focused on the dog, a mix of Great Dane with Rottweiler he'd guess, and shook his head. "He's not one of my patients, and isn't familiar." He approached the dog and let him sniff his fingers before petting the dog and running his hand along his neck. "He might be microchipped so I could find the owner that way."

"Good. Starr gave me one of the office's

leashes since he didn't have one on him."
She peered at Jack. "Are you okay?"

Did his grief over the cat show? "I'm
expecting bad news about one of my favorite patients."

"I'm sorry, Jack." She reached out and
rubbed his arm before she dropped her
hand to her side, as if realizing that she
might be overstepping. "Well, I should go."
She pulled her purse strap higher on her
shoulder and walked to the door.

"How have you been?" He didn't want
her to leave just yet. This was the first
time he'd seen her since Halloween, and
he didn't want the moment to pass without trying to fix their relationship. Even if
he wasn't sure how to go about doing that.

She gave a shrug. "Fine."

They gazed at each other in silence until
Mel looked away.

"About the other night—"

She shook her head. "I've got to go."

"We need to talk about this."

"I'm not ready yet."

"I don't want to lose you, Mel."

She closed her eyes and took a deep
breath. "I'm getting a makeover."

Jack wasn't sure what that had to do with their friendship. "Why?"

"And I'm going on a date. More than one actually."

"Good for you."

Mel nodded. "Yes, it will be." She glanced at the dog. "You'll let me know if you find the owner?"

"You brought him to the right place."

"I know. You've always been so good at helping dogs find the right homes."

Once she walked out the door, the dog started to howl. Jack put a hand on his head. "It's okay, fella. She'll be back."

But the dog continued to howl and strain on the leash to follow Mel. Since the dog weighed at least a hundred pounds, he soon broke free from Jack's grasp and ran after Mel. Jack followed and found the dog blocking the exit door, Mel trying to negotiate with him.

She turned and said, "Did you put him up to this?"

"He seems to like you." Jack couldn't blame the dog's good taste.

She patted the dog's head, but he wouldn't step aside. "I have to go." She tugged on the leash, but the dog stayed where he was. "Jack, want to give me a hand here?"

Jack took hold of the leash, but the dog still refused to move from blocking the door. "Looks like he doesn't want you to leave."

"Well, I can't stay."

"I've heard of animals forming an attachment like this to a stranger, but I haven't seen a dog so determined to be with you."

Melanie paled at his words. "Be with me? I can't have a dog."

"You can, but you choose not to."

Mel glanced between Jack and the dog. "This is ridiculous. He belongs to somebody, so you have to find who it is. But it's definitely not me."

"Would you be willing to care for him while I search for his owners?"

Mel pursed her lips together as she stared at the dog, then crouched down so she was eye level with him. "You don't want to stay with me. I don't have any dog food or toys at my house."

"I can give you some." He had plenty in

his office that would help her get started to care for the dog.

Mel looked up at him. "And I'm on the cusp of starting the busiest season of the year at the store. What am I going to do with a dog while I'm working?" She folded her arms, as if defiant, and the dog moved forward to rest his head on her shoulder.

Mel resisted touching the dog, but only for a moment before she put her arms around him and rubbed his back between the shoulder blades. "You don't want to be with me."

"I think he does." Jack crouched down beside them. "You can always bring him here while you're at the store. Lucas is starting a doggy daycare in the empty store space next to ours. You can drop him off in the morning, then pick him up at the end of the day."

"But this is only temporary."

Jack nodded and petted the dog. "Sure. Only until we find the owner."

"And if you can't?"

"Then I'll find a new family that does want a dog."

MEL FELT AS if she were on display as Kristina Cuthbert circled her and let her eyes roam up from her feet to the top of her head. "Hmm. You've given me a lot to work with." Kristina looked into her eyes and squinted. "How much time did you say I have?"

"My first date is set up for tomorrow night at six?" Mel said it as if it was a question. Mostly because she kept wondering why she'd agreed to meet Emma's next-door neighbor. But her assistant at the bookshop insisted that he was a nice guy. And cute on top of that.

Kristina gaped at her in mock horror. "Are you expecting miracles in less than twenty-four hours?" She gestured at Mel in the mirror. "I can make you presentable for that at least. Making you a knockout will take more time. What are the plans?"

"We're meeting at this Chinese restaurant the next town over."

"He's not picking you up for dinner?" Kristina rubbed the space between her carefully manicured eyebrows. "I see that I have much to teach you."

Shelby had recommended her fashion-

forward cousin to help Mel with her makeover efforts. Kristina's makeup and fashion
skills were evidently legendary. But standing in the woman's bedroom made Mel
doubt that she was ready for this. An ex-
plosion of colorful dresses lay on the bed
surrounded by various shoes, some that
looked like torture devices with thin
spiked heels. Mel bent over to pick one up
and tried to imagine her foot inside its thin
straps. Kristina plucked the shoe from her
hands. "You're not quite ready for that yet."

Mel clasped her hands in front of her.
"We're just having dinner."

Kristina's eyebrow rose. "There is no
such thing as just dinner when you're serious about dating. You need to approach
this like a job interview. Be prepared and
ready because you never know when you
might get a long-term offer."

"Is he interviewing me? Or am I interviewing him?"

"It should be mutual, but I've discovered
that the best men are more eager to know
more about you than to talk about themselves." Kristina waved away the question. "But that's neither here nor there. I

think for tonight, we should focus on your appearance. The rest of what you need to know will come with time."

She put a hand on the clip that held up Mel's hair and released it, the long brown strands falling around her shoulders. Kristina fingered the clip, nodding. "You've never colored your hair?"

Mel had never seen a reason to. She shook her head. "It's the same color I've had since I was born. Is that wrong?"

"You've got beautiful natural golden highlights mixed in with the brown. Keeps it from being too mousy." Kristina took a fistful of her hair and held it above Mel's head before releasing it and letting it fall in a cascade. "How do you feel about cutting it?"

Mel reached up and clutched the hair to her chest. "But I've always worn it long."

"Exactly. I think it's time for a change, don't you? Isn't that why you sought out my advice?" Kristina nodded as she turned Mel's face side to side. "The long hair dwarfs your face, and we can't see your beautiful brown eyes and gorgeous cheekbones. You're hiding them when some women would do almost anything to have them." She shook her head. "No, you need something shorter. Lighter. Lots of layers. But not too short. At least not this first time. I'm thinking your hair should skim your shoulders."

Mel nodded, knowing she was right. "You're the expert."

Kristina smiled then, and Mel knew she was in trouble.

Hours later, after Kristina had cut and styled her hair, dressed her in an outfit and applied makeup, Mel stared into her reflection in the closet door mirror. Was she really the woman staring back at her? Kristina entered the mirror's reflection as she stood behind Mel and smiled. "It's amazing what a little mousse and eyeliner can do, isn't it?"

But it was more than just the cosmetics that had brought out this transformation. Mel's hair now hung to her shoulders in soft waves that Kristina had shown her how to recreate with a round brush and hair dryer. It was also the sapphire dress that clung to her curves and the short black heels on her feet. Mel put a hand to her waist and marveled at how she suddenly had an hourglass figure. "I can't believe how you made me look."

"I only worked with what you have. And, Melanie, this is just the beginning. Shelby told me to go full makeover with you, so that's what I'm planning. You've got the haircut, but now we need to update your cosmetics and wardrobe. When's the next date after tomorrow night?"

Mel stopped staring at her reflection and blinked, mentally reviewing her calendar. "I'm meeting someone for drinks after work on Monday."

Again, Kristina sighed and shook her head. "Let me guess. He's meeting you at the bar. If a man doesn't make an effort from the start, then when will he? Going forward, you make your date pick you up."

"The books I've been reading said to meet the first time in a public place."

Kristina wrinkled her nose. "Books?" She rolled her eyes. "You're talking to someone who has had an active social life since I was fourteen. I'm telling you from personal experience that if you want to find something that lasts with a man, you have him pick you up at your house. And if you're not comfortable with him being at your house, then have him meet you at your store and drive you from there."

Mel wasn't sure about that advice since what Kristina said contradicted everything she'd been reading lately. And her reading list was exhaustive. After tossing the friend zone book to the side, she had purchased a pile of books that she was working through and now sat on her nightstand in her bedroom. Another mound at the kitchen table that she perused as she ate her meals. And a third stack at the store in the back room where she took her break. "Well, I appreciate the advice. And the loan of the clothes."

"This is just the beginning, Mel. I'll transform you into a woman that men will fight to be near. And I'll get you enough dates to make sure that you'll never spend another evening alone."

MEL GLANCED AT her watch and winced. Only two minutes since the last time she'd checked. Where was this guy?

When Mel had mentioned to Emma that she was interested in getting set up with eligible men, her employee had mentioned the man who lived next door to her. "He's really nice. And cute too, if you're into puppy dog eyes and hair that tends to get too long before he gets it cut."

"As long as he's single."

So Emma had given Stuart her phone number, and he'd called that following evening. Two phone calls later, and they agreed to meet.

Only he was ten minutes late and counting.

The server stopped at her table and re-filled her water glass. "Is your companion on his way?"

Mel certainly hoped so. She scanned the dinner crowd at the restaurant, wondering if she was doing the right thing. Well, she'd give him another five minutes and then she'd leave. After ordering takeout, of course, since the restaurant's moo shu pork was one of her favorites. The night shouldn't be a complete waste after all.

She took a sip of her water, her eyes drawn to the front of the restaurant as the door opened. She sighed. It was a tall man following a shorter woman who must be his mother. Definitely not her date.

Until the woman stopped at her table. "Melanie Beach?"

Mel gave a short nod, then began to protest as the woman slid into the bench seat across from her. "I'm expecting someone."

"Yes. My son Stuart." The woman motioned to the tall man who took a seat next to his mother.

"Hey there." Stuart shot her a quick smile, then grabbed the menu, flinging open its bright red leather cover.

Mel turned to the woman. "I'm sorry, Mrs. Brocklehurst. I didn't realize you were joining us for dinner since Stuart never mentioned it." She racked her memory to see if she had been mistaken, but in the two phone conversations he hadn't referenced his mother once.

"Stuart is shy when he meets women for the first time, so I come along to help him out. Give him a hand. He's a real catch, just not great with conversation. In person." She picked up her menu. "I hear the sweet and sour shrimp is fabulous here."

This night certainly wasn't starting out

as Mel had expected. Not that she had much experience in the dating world to draw from. Maybe she should text Kristina to see if this was typical dating behavior, but she doubted it. And there had been nothing about mothers accompanying their sons on dates in any of the books she'd read.

Following her dinner companions' example, Mel likewise picked up her menu and perused the different entrées but settled on the moo shu pork in the end.

Once they ordered their meals and their server left, silence descended on the table. Mel looked at Stuart, silently imploring him to say something. Frankly, she was at a loss.

Emma had been right about Stuart's puppy dog eyes, but she'd failed to mention his bulldog of a mother. Mel had to try something, the silence was too much to bear. "So, Stuart, you said you work for the post office."

"Been there fifteen years too. Got a special commendation from the mayor of Thora and everything," said his mother, looking pleased as punch.

"Mom," Stuart said, his cheeks burning. "You don't have to keep bringing that up."

"And why not? It's something to be proud of."

He leaned past his mother and shrugged in Melanie's direction. "It wasn't that big of a deal."

"No big deal? He single-handedly delivered all of Thora's mail during the blizzard of 2012."

Mel remembered hearing about the single mail carrier who had delivered the mail during the biggest snowfall in Thora's history. "That was you?"

Stuart looked at her before giving a soft nod.

"And you've always lived in Thora?" she asked, holding his gaze.

"His whole life," Mrs. Brocklehurst promptly replied. "He kindly moved in with me a few years back. I had to have a hip replacement operation, and Stuart was gracious enough to help care for me while I healed." His mother took one of the napkins off the table and handed it to Stuart, who cringed and placed it in his lap.

"Ah." He definitely hadn't mentioned

any of that in his calls. It showed that he had a kind heart if he would give up his time to care for his mother. Though the fact that it had been years since and he hadn't moved out caused some concern. The dating books said to pay attention to red flags, and that was surely one of them.

Mrs. Brocklehurst, smiling, straightened in her chair. "He'd be a good provider for the right woman."

Mel didn't need the rest of the night to doubt very sincerely that she was that woman. Stuart had seemed sort of nerdy cool during their phone conversations, but how this evening was unfolding told her all she needed to know. This was one mama's boy who had to cut those apron strings soon if he wanted to find any kind of long-term relationship. And Melanie was not the woman to help him do that.

Mel fiddled with her silverware. This was her first dip into the dating pool, and she wondered if she was ready after all.

"Stuart says you own a bookstore."

"Mel's Books on Main Street. Have you ever been?"

The woman cocked her head to one

side. "You're next to the candle store? I've walked by that place but have never come in."

"You should the next time you're on Main. Do you like to read?"

Stuart's mother sighed. "I used to read for hours, but I've gotten too busy until recently. I retired from Bailey and Brothers Accounting a few months ago, so I have more time for myself now."

"Who's your favorite author?"

The women talked favorite books as Stuart sat, watching them. Mel knew from their previous conversations that he didn't care much for books, which she'd promised not to hold against him. Now she wondered what else she'd overlooked in order to meet him. By the time their meals came, Stuart's mother, Edith, had agreed to stop by and check out Mel's latest romance novels as well as attend the monthly book club meeting.

Stuart looked at his mother. "I think I can handle this from here, Mom. Thanks."

Edith pointed to the empty table next to theirs and asked the waiter, "Do you mind if I eat at that table? These kids need their privacy."

Mel almost regretted Edith's retreat to the other table, but appreciated the sentiment. Mel took a bite of her moo shu, savoring the pop of flavor in her mouth. "This is *really* good. How's your dinner?"

Stuart seemed uncertain and then shrugged.

Okay. New topic. "Your mom seems super nice."

"She is."

"I wish you had told me she was coming with you tonight."

"I know it's not conventional to bring my mother along on our date, but I've been burned before because I'm not a good judge of people."

"You still should have mentioned it."

He agreed. "She seems to like you. That's a point in your favor."

Conversation between them continued while they ate, but Mel knew that she wouldn't be seeking a second date with Stuart. He seemed like a nice guy, but he wasn't for her.

She focused on her meal, eating enough

to be social, but soon requested a carryout box to take the rest home. Once she received the box, she opened her wallet and placed money on the table. "This should cover my dinner."

Stuart frowned. "You're leaving already?"

Mel winced. She rose to her feet and grabbed her leftovers that she would save for her lunch tomorrow. "I told you that I have an early morning at the store. It was..." She couldn't say *pleasant* or *nice*. She wouldn't lie. But she had to say something. "...interesting meeting you both." If anything, it had helped her dip a toe into the dating pool. It was a start, and she'd chalk it up to experience. She gave a wide smile. "Enjoy your evening."

She was halfway to her car when she heard her name being called. Turning, she found Edith chasing after her. "Melanie, wait." What the woman had to say to her she couldn't guess, but she waited for her to approach. "I hope you'll give my son another chance. He really likes you."

"Are you sure? There wasn't a lot of, uh, well, chemistry between us."

"I know my son. And he likes you."
She glanced around the parking lot. "I
also know it was unconventional for me
to come with him tonight on your date, but
I've discovered that I'm a better judge of
people than he is. And I don't want to see
him get hurt again."

"I appreciate your candor, so I hope you
will appreciate mine." She almost dropped
her takeout box but saved it at the last moment. "I'm not interested in your son, Mrs.
Brocklehurst. Oh, sorry, I mean Edith. But
it was lovely to talk books with you. I wish
you both the best."

Mel turned on her heel and wobbled
slightly before striding the rest of her way
to the car. She tried to think of someone
who might be a match for Stuart as she
pulled out of the parking lot.

When she got home, she texted Shelby
the details of her disastrous date, then hov-
ered over Jack's name in the text history.
If it had been a week ago, she might have
texted him too. He would laugh with her
over it and encourage her to keep trying.
That the right man was out there.

But she couldn't text him. Couldn't call.

Instead, she closed her phone, then sat on her sofa and stared out the living room window.

"JACK XAVIER CUTHBERT, you haven't heard a word I've said."

Jack looked up at his great-aunt Sarah who peered at him from the other end of the sofa. She'd caught him. At her request, he had come to visit her apartment at the seniors' home, but his mind was a million miles elsewhere. He ducked his head. "Sorry. Something's been on my mind."

"Something? Or someone?"

Her eyes seemed to sparkle, and he knew what she was thinking. He loved his great-aunt, but Sarah tended to think of herself as the family matchmaker. She claimed that she'd set up Penny with her husband, and she was right about that. If she hadn't insisted that Penny move in with her when Christopher's family did after a house fire, the two would never have met. The fact that she said she'd set up Josh and Shelby was a bit more involved. After all, they'd known each other since high school and reconnected when he moved back to town. That gleam in her eyes meant she was ready to start matching him up with some woman who he figured would only leave him in the end.

And maybe he had been thinking about little else than Melanie and her confession since Halloween. But Aunt Sarah didn't need to know that. He gave her a shrug. "Just something minor."

"Well, something's on my mind too, which is why I asked you here this evening." She stood and crossed the tiny apartment to grab a plastic container from her kitchen counter. She opened it, then held it out to him. "Maybe if you eat one of my snickerdoodle cookies it will put you in a better frame of mind."

He took one and bit into it, then frowned as he chewed. "I didn't know you had the time to bake cookies. You always seem so active now, especially since you don't have the big house to look after anymore. You never seem to be home when I call you."

Aunt Sarah held out the cookie container to her fiancé, Mr. Duffy, who took three snickerdoodles and winked at her before she settled beside him on the sofa.

"That's true, but I've always liked baking. It's a methodical process, helps me think. Clear my mind. You should maybe try it." She took a cookie herself, then placed the cookie container on the coffee table and within arm's reach.

He peered at her, wondering if she had heard about Mel's feelings for him. Thora was a suburb, but it felt more like a small town and news tended to get around fast, especially in his family. "This isn't about Melanie, is it? Because I'm not going along with your matchmaking."

Aunt Sarah put a hand on her chest, and her mouth dropped open. "I take offense at that. I'm much too busy planning my own wedding to meddle in your love life." She patted Mr. Duffy's hand before she sat up a little straighter. "Even if you could use my help with that woman—you know, you're going to lose her if you don't watch it."

"We're just friends, Aunt Sarah. That's all."

"I know that's what you think. And that's why I've set her up with a guy I know."

Jack peered at her. "You set Mel up on a date?"

"She said she was interested in meeting someone, so I gave her the phone number of a nice single guy I know. Is that a problem?"

He took a second cookie from the plastic container to avoid answering her. "You didn't ask me here to talk about Mel."

She huffed and straightened the hem of her blouse. "No, I didn't." She raised her eyes to look at him. She reached over to take Mr. Duffy's hand in hers. "You know that I'm getting married on New Year's Day, and I'm too involved in planning the wedding to take on anything else right now. So I want you to take my place on the family's planning committee for the annual Christmas fundraiser."

Every December, the Cuthbert family hosted a dinner and dance to raise money to provide gifts for children in the community who might not get a Christmas otherwise. His great-grandfather had started the tradition almost a hundred years before, and it had become an annual event ever since.

But chairing the event was not something he could commit to. "No."

"You haven't heard me out yet."

"You'd have been better off convincing me to ask Mel out on a date." He raised his hands. "But neither one's going to happen." He got off the sofa and walked into the kitchenette, noticing that a picture of Mr. Duffy now graced the counter. Another change that he didn't know how to process. His great-aunt had never married, and he'd figured that she was happy and settled as a single person. But Mr. Duffy had changed all that.

"I need you on that committee."

He turned back to face his great-aunt. "You know how unpredictable my schedule is at the animal clinic. I can't commit to what would be required for such an undertaking. I can double the donation I gave last year, but I don't have the time to do this."

"It's important that one of you kids take the lead on this. After all, this is a Cuthbert family tradition, and a Cuthbert needs to be involved in planning the fundraiser."

"So ask Shelby. She did it last year."

"She's still in Greece. But when she returns, she'll be working with you on the fundraiser."

"Then ask another one of my cousins. I have plenty to choose from." He stepped back toward the sofa. "I can't do it."

Aunt Sarah pursed her lips. "Honestly, you weren't my first choice, but I'm running out of options. And I think this would be good for you."

"I don't see how."

Aunt Sarah patted the sofa next to her. "Would you mind sitting down? I'm getting a crick in my neck having to look up at you."

Jack sighed, but took a seat once again next to her. They sat quietly, the only sound in the apartment the ticking of a clock on the wall. He peered at it, remembering when it had once hung in Nana and Pops's kitchen at the old Cuthbert house. The one that his cousin Penny and her new husband and family now lived in. Things couldn't stay the same forever, and the house seemed to be one more of those things. As much as he might have wanted it to never change, it had. And now Great-aunt Sarah lived in the seniors' home and would soon marry Mr. Duffy.

He didn't want things to change. What was so wrong with being comfortable in the status quo? But if he had learned anything the last week and a half it was that nothing stayed the same. Not his family. Not even his relationship with Mel. She still wasn't talking to him, and he missed her more than he thought he might have. So many times, he'd reached for his phone to send her a message. And just as quickly put it back down. She'd made it clear that she didn't want to hear from him, and he was honoring her request for space. Even if he disagreed that it was helping either one of them.

He sighed and placed one leg on top of his knee. "If I agree, and I'm saying this is a big if, what would I have to do?"

Aunt Sarah grinned and pulled out a binder with a cracked spine. "Most of it is right here, so it's not that big of a deal." She handed the binder to him. "It's just updating details with the vendors. Confirming the dates. Getting posters and tickets printed for the event. Securing the corporate donors. Much of the groundwork has already been taken care of."

Jack groaned as he flipped through the pages. "This *is* a big deal. And it's a lot of work that I don't have time for." He looked over at his aunt. "How am I supposed to fit this in with everything else going on right now?"

"Oh? I hadn't heard that you're in a relationship. Or even have a social life."

He eyed her. "You know the answer to that. And I do have a social life." Although a large part of it had been with Mel who wanted nothing to do with him at the moment and Shelby who was traveling. He'd been spending more time alone at home lately which he didn't particularly enjoy.

"This will help you find a balance. That's why this would be perfect for you."

Somehow, he doubted that. If anything, he was going to be swamped with patients at the clinic and scrambling at the end to get this event planned. "I can't do this on my own."

"That's why there's a committee, so you won't be alone. The first meeting is this Wednesday night at eight at the library, and I expect you to be there and represent the family."

He groaned, but found himself agreeing. He never could tell Aunt Sarah no.

THE NOISE OF the sports bar and grill drowned out any misgivings Mel might be having about meeting her date there. Televisions blared the football game and the basketball game and competed with the music playing over the sound system. If nothing else, any awkward silences between her and Clay would be filled with other noise.

She took a seat at the bar and waited for her date. He'd said he'd be there by eight, and it was five minutes before. She had originally thought she was going to be late because while they closed the store, she had been answering Emma's questions about why her prior night out hadn't been successful. "It was a disaster for a few reasons," Mel had told her.

Emma gave a shrug. "Sorry. He seems like a nice guy, and you deserve someone who is nice."

"I think I convinced his mother to join

our book club, so that was something good at least, to have come out of the evening."

Emma sighed. "Fair enough. Hey, what about—"

"Is that you, Melanie?"

From her spot at the bar, Mel turned to see an attractive man wearing a suit and tie. She felt a little underdressed in the twinset sweater and skirt that she'd worn to work. At least she'd changed into heels like Kristina had insisted. She smiled and held out her hand. "You must be Clay."

They shook hands, and she noted that he had a firm, confident grip. He nodded toward a quiet area of the bar. "Do you mind sitting over there? We might be able to hear each other better, away from all this activity."

Score a few points for Clay. Melanie followed him to a table where he pulled out the chair for her. That earned him a few more. She thanked him before taking a seat. "It's good to see that chivalry hasn't died."

"There's no reason to not have good manners." He took the seat across from her, then handed her a menu that was wedged between the napkin dispenser and bottle of ketchup. "I know we said we'd meet just for drinks, but I haven't had a chance to eat all day. Would you mind sharing an appetizer combo?"

Mel agreed, then glanced around the bar, checking to make sure his mother wasn't waiting to join them. When it appeared that they were alone, she took a deep breath and felt herself relaxing into the chair. So far, this was going pretty well.

When the server approached the table, Clay ordered the appetizers as well as their drinks. Beer for him. A strawberry daiquiri for her. Shortly after, her drink arrived with his, and Clay touched the edge of her glass with the bottle of his beer. "Here's to a nice evening of getting to know each other."

Melanie smiled and took a sip of her daiquiri. "Sarah said that you were successful, but never mentioned what you do for a living."

"I'm a financial adviser. That's how I met her. I did an estate planning seminar at the seniors' home where she lives, and we got to talking after my presentation."

He shook his head, but gave a wide smile. "She's quite a character, isn't she?"

"That she is. She's always been special to me."

"When she said she knew an attractive woman she wanted me to meet, I figured that she was probably exaggerating." He peered at her, letting his gaze linger the longest over her face before drifting to her shoulders. "But I don't think she gave you enough credit. You're a beautiful woman, Melanie."

Mel felt her cheeks burning. She wasn't sure what to say, but was saved from having to say anything when the waiter dropped off a large platter of appetizers at the table before whisking away with a pizza for another table. The waiter reappeared a moment later with two small plates. "Do we need a refresh on the drinks?"

Mel shook her head since she'd had only a few sips of her drink, but Clay ordered another beer. The waiter strode off again.

Clay motioned to the platter. "Help yourself. Their mozzarella sticks are out of this world."

She took a few things from the large

selection and placed them on the plate before her, but she wasn't really hungry. To be polite, she tried a cheese stick. "They are good."

Clay smiled and dipped his into the marinara sauce. "Sarah mentioned that you own your own business."

"Mel's Books on Main Street. Maybe you've heard of it?"

"I don't read much beyond the stock exchange and the financial websites."

"I can't imagine a day without reading a book, but then I guess that's why I'm in the business that I am."

"And your store does what? About half a million in sales a year?"

Mel almost choked on her drink and grabbed a napkin to dab her mouth before saying, "Excuse me?"

"I'm just curious. How many books do you sell annually?"

An interesting question for a first date, but maybe he was trying to assess if she was successful and had a drive as strong as his own. "Enough. I make a decent living. I mean, I'm an independent book seller in a world that thrives on online shopping, so I'm not nearly making Amazon numbers."

Clay nodded and drained his first beer before starting the second. "And you've got insurance in case of emergencies, right? Fire? Water damage? Theft? And then life insurance for yourself?"

Mel pushed her plate away from the edge of the table, not liking the direction of his questioning. "I don't understand where this conversation is going."

"Let me be blunt with you." Clay set his bottle of beer to the side. "I'm very good at helping people like you make sure that their insurance needs are met. Like I helped your aunt Sarah."

"She's not really my aunt."

"Regardless, I'd like to set up a time where we can go over a portfolio that will not only protect your business presently, but help you achieve the future that you envision for yourself. Including your retirement."

It was very clear that any future she might have was not going to include this guy. Mel scraped back her chair. "Wait. Are you here to sell me insurance?"

Clay looked at her as she grabbed her coat and purse from the back of the chair. "You're leaving already?"

"I don't see any need to keep the conversation going if all you're here to do is sell me something that I don't want or need. Do you? Because then we'd both be wasting our time."

He at least had the common sense to look sheepish. "When I'm nervous, I fall back on what I do well, which is sales." He stood and pulled out her chair and motioned to it with his hand. "Please. Let's start this over."

She looked at him for a long time before giving a soft nod. "Besides sales, what else are you good at?"

He smiled as if he couldn't wait to tell her. "I'm great at golf. Do you play?"

JACK ARRIVED EARLY for the committee meeting. Aunt Sarah had reserved the conference room at the Thora library, and he was the first to arrive. He placed the worn binder on the table and took a seat, tapping his fingers against the table. Aunt Sarah hadn't mentioned who else would be showing up. Or how many. Whoever did would have to understand that he would do what was required, but likely not more than that. Bottom line, it was important that the Cuthbert family be involved. He'd get the planning started, then hand it over to Shelby when she returned from her vacation. That was a compromise he could live with.

The door opened, and he stood as an attractive woman entered. "Sorry I'm late. I had a last-minute customer that had a book emergency."

She unbuttoned her coat and laid it over the back of a chair, then turned and stared at him across the table. "What are you doing here, Jack?"

Was the woman standing in front of him really Mel? She looked different. He stared at her, hard. She'd cut her hair. And was she wearing eyeliner? She didn't usually wear makeup. He let his eyes wander down from her face and noticed her clothes. "What are you wearing?"

Mel looked down at the emerald wrap dress with a V collar that revealed more than she normally would. "It's called a dress."

"But you never wear dresses."

She seemed to bristle at his words. "I do now."

"Why are you here? This is the committee meeting for the Cuthbert annual fundraiser." He said the words, hoping that the sinking feeling in his stomach was wrong.

She took a seat across the table from him and opened a notebook. "Shelby's still in Greece, so she asked me to take her place as cochair on the committee until she returns. Why are you here?"

Jack opened and closed his mouth before shaking his head. He should have known his aunt had ulterior motives for getting him to take her spot. "Aunt Sarah asked me to take her place as cochair on the committee."

"Ah."

"What does that mean?"

Mel sighed and looked around the room, empty except for the two of them. "They're plotting to get us back together."

"Back together?" She talked as if they were a couple who had broken up. Okay, so maybe their friendship had taken a pause while they reassessed what they wanted, but they hadn't dated. Would never date.

"You know what I mean."

He frowned. "I'm not the one who didn't want to be friends anymore. You're the one who asked for space."

Mel put her coat back on. "This isn't going to work. You don't get it. Please apologize to your cousin and your aunt, but I can't work with you."

Then she left the conference room as Jack wondered what in the world had happened to the woman who had been his best friend.

CHAPTER FOUR

MELANIE WEAVED HER way through book-shelves as she tried to exit the library. To-night was just another prime example of how off track her life had become. She should be able to have a civil conversation with Jack, but even that didn't seem possible anymore. What had gone so wrong?

Someone pulled on her arm, and she turned to face Jack. "Don't leave, Mel."

"There's no point in my being here." She tugged her arm free.

A librarian came around the corner to shush them. Mel apologized and tried to walk outside, but Jack followed. "Come back to the conference room with me. Let's talk about this."

She kept walking.

Jack stayed where he was. "You can't even stand to be in the same room with me?" He closed his eyes. "What happened to us?"

He'd broken her heart is what happened. Did he not realize that? She couldn't be around him as if nothing had happened. "I have to go."

He opened his eyes to gaze at her. "You planned on working on the fundraiser this evening, so you don't have any other plans. Where else could you possibly have to be?"

Anywhere but here with Jack.

But he was right. She'd agreed to work on the committee to help out Shelby, and she wasn't one who didn't follow through on her commitments. "Fine. But we're only going to discuss the fundraiser. Nothing else."

When he agreed, she strode past Jack back to the conference room and took the seat she'd recently abandoned. She crossed her arms as Jack entered the room. He took a seat across from her and opened the binder. "It looks as if Aunt Sarah and Shelby have laid down most of the framework for the event. When everyone else arrives, we'll need to delegate responsibilities and go from there." He didn't say a word, but his gaze landed on her new hair and face. He colored slightly as if caught staring and cleared his throat before asking, "How does that sound?"

The door to the conference room opened to usher in Jack's cousin Olivia, chatting with another member of the committee, who Mel recognized as a customer from the bookstore.

For the next hour, they discussed the upcoming dinner and dance that would be the bulk of their fundraising efforts. Jack reviewed with them what was already in place and made a list of things that still needed to be confirmed or purchased. Mel assigned tasks to each person, including taking on the job of procuring what they'd need for the wreath sale that coincided with the dance.

When the librarian knocked, letting them know the library was closing, Olivia was the first to stand and slip into her coat. She looked at Jack. "We should probably meet again next week. Same place and time?"

He gave a short nod. "We should probably plan to meet weekly until the night of the dinner dance." He looked at everyone else. "Sound good?"

They all agreed. As Olivia started to leave, she put a hand on Mel's arm. "You and Jack make a really good team. This is the smoothest first committee meeting I've been to, and I've helped with this thing for the last six years." She turned and winked at Jack. "See ya, cuz."

Mel tried to smile at the compliment, but the words only fanned the disappointment she already felt. She took her time putting on her coat and reaching for her purse so that she was left alone with Jack.

He handed her the binder. "Despite everything else going on between us at the moment, my cousin's right. We make a good team, Mel. We always have."

Mel closed her eyes. "You can't say things like that."

"It's the truth. We've always worked well together. That hasn't changed."

She opened her eyes and looked at him. Nothing had changed for him, even if she still nursed her bruised heart. "But other things have, and I can't go back to the way we were. I don't care how well we work together, you and I can't be friends right now."

She walked out of the conference room, her steps quick and purposeful, trying to get as far from Jack as she could. But he'd been a track star in high school and caught up to her at the exit door of the library. "Can I say something without you biting my head off?"

"No." She studied his face and wished for the thousandth time that the sight of it didn't make her heart beat faster. "I don't think you understand how hurt I am."

"I can't make myself feel something that I don't, Mel. And it's not fair for you to hold that against me." He caught her gaze and held it. "I wanted to tell you how much I miss you. Miss our texts and phone calls. You're the only person I want to talk to before I go to bed every night."

Tears pricked her eyes, but she wouldn't cry. Not again. And especially not in front of Jack. Instead, she set her jaw in a determined grimace. "I miss you too, but I can't pretend anymore."

"So what am I supposed to do to fix this? Tell me, and I swear it's done."

She looked at him, knowing that he meant it. He would do anything for her.

Anything but love her.

"I don't know, Jack. But right now, I'm asking you to leave me alone."

"Anything but that."

She hit the key fob to unlock her car doors, and she sighed as she shook her head. "You're going to have to try."

MEL PUT A finger in the book she was reading to keep her spot and glanced up at the customer who had thrown a shadow over her page. "Marius, you came back."

He stood in front of her and put his arms akimbo, pushing aside the edges of his coat. "I wasn't sure you'd remember me."

His smile made her return one of her own. "Well, of course I'd remember a vampire that works at the hospital." She placed her book aside. "Did you need help with something again?"

"The books you picked out for my nephew were a huge hit. Got any more like them?"

"Do I?" She laughed and walked around

the counter, crooking her finger at him to follow her to the children's section.

She plucked several selections off the shelves as she strode through and placed them on the table in the section before leaving to retrieve a few more. Marius's eyebrows rose into his hairline. "That many?"

"And these are just the ones I have on hand. I can special order at least a dozen or more different authors with stories like these."

"Maybe we could discuss them over dinner tonight. All for my nephew's benefit, of course."

Her smile faded. "Unfortunately, I already have plans." She'd made arrangements to meet an interesting prospect she'd met online. Since the introductions to single men from friends didn't seem to be working out, she'd turned to online dating as a solution. So far, her profile had turned up several promising possibilities.

"So ditch the plans and have dinner with me." He waggled his eyebrows.

She looked him over. Without his pale makeup and drip of fake blood in the corner of his mouth, Marius looked good. He was still in scrubs, so he must have come over to the store right from the hospital. His kind eyes and amazing smile snagged her interest again. She might have better luck with him than she had with the other first dates. She shrugged. "Sorry. Not tonight."

"Meaning you will another night?"

Mel gave a soft nod. "Fine. You've worn me down. Another night."

Marius pumped a fist in the air. "I knew this was going to be a good day. How does Saturday night work for you? A buddy of mine plays in a jazz trio, and they're appearing at this restaurant in downtown Detroit. What do you say?"

"I'd say that sounds like a date."

Marius gave her a bright smile, and she found herself looking forward to it far more than her date that evening.

THE SHIH TZU on the exam table peered up at Jack with a forlorn expression. "I know, Caesar. I feel the same way."

His cousin Penny looked at him from across the table, her eyebrows knit together. "So what's wrong with him?"

Jack gave Caesar a pat on his back. "He's constipated. What have you been feeding him?"

"Dog food."

Jack raised an eyebrow at this. "Just the dog food?" When she didn't answer, he shook his head. "What else, Pen?"

"He loves cheese like me, so I give him some every time I open the refrigerator. He jumps up and whines until I give him some." She put a hand under Caesar's face and scratched his chin. "I can't resist that little face."

"You'll have to start resisting. His weight is up since his last visit, and all that cheese is causing digestive issues for the little guy."

"Fine. I'll be stricter with him. What can we do for him now though?"

"I'll give you a stool softener, which should help." He removed his gloves, then reached into the lab coat pocket to retrieve his prescription pad. "And I'd lay off on the people food until we get his weight back where it should be. The excess pounds will put too much pressure on his knees as he gets older. Speaking of his age, do you know how old he is?"

Penny scrunched up her face. "I'd have to check with Christopher. He came to the family as a stray just after his wife died, so I doubt he knows for sure."

Jack handed her the prescription. "How is married life going?" His cousin had gotten married at the end of August, and she seemed to be happy.

She smiled as if she knew an amazing secret. "No complaints."

"And Christopher's kids? They're okay with you stepping into their family?"

"Sure, we've had some bumps, but we're on the same page. We've made a good connection. I love those kids." She picked Caesar up in her arms and placed him on the floor, holding his leash. "I can't believe I've known them all less than a year, but what a year it's been." She peered at him. "What about you? Seeing anyone? Mel maybe?"

"No maybe about Mel. She's on this self-improvement kick. Cut her hair. Wearing dresses. She's asked everyone to set her up on dates. Even Aunt Sarah." He shook his head. "It's like I don't even know her anymore."

"Good for Mel. It's about time she did something to find someone. But what about you? Are you looking for anyone?"

"Work keeps me too busy."

"That's just an excuse you use to avoid taking a risk."

"I'd say that Caesar would tell you that my focus on work means dogs like him can thrive."

Penny scoffed, but didn't push him on it. "Thanksgiving dinner is at our house again, and I expect you to be there. Maybe you could buy a couple of pies and bring them?"

"I will."

"And tell Mel that she's welcome to join us. Just like always."

He nodded as he opened the door to allow Penny and Caesar to leave the exam room. Mel usually joined him and his family for the holidays since her dad and step-mom lived most of the year in Florida and didn't make the trip up to see her often. But he wasn't sure she would want to join them now that she was putting distance between them.

"I'll ask her."

"Good. And maybe finally ask her out on a date while you're at it."

"We're just friends." Why couldn't his family accept that?

"And that's why you'll lose her eventually. Everyone else can see that the two of you are meant to be together. Why can't you?"

MEL UNLOCKED HER front door and let the dog enter first. Despite several attempts at keeping him off the sofa, he went straight for it as usual and jumped up and sat, and was now waiting for her to join him. She walked to the couch and collapsed onto it before removing the heels from her feet. Massaging her feet, she groaned. Some from the relief of getting her feet out of the torture devices, but more from the disaster of another date. They'd met at the same sports bar and grill she'd met Clay at, but he'd been more interested in the football game on the screen than in talking with her. She'd left the bar at halftime, but she doubted that he'd noticed. What had she been thinking when she'd agreed to meet this guy?

She'd been thinking of what Jack would say if he knew that she was dating someone else. Hoping that he'd see her as a woman and be jealous. After all, wasn't that why she was doing this?

No, she was seeking out men to find a companion. Someone she could spend holidays with. Marry and have a family with. Grow old together.

The joke was on her though. None of the dates had gone well, and Jack didn't seem to care whether or not she was seeing someone else. He was suspicious of her new wardrobe and disliked her haircut, but that seemed to be the extent of his reaction to her makeover efforts.

Besides, she realized that he was right. He couldn't pretend to love her just so she would feel better. He couldn't make himself feel something for her when he didn't. And that's why these dates were important for her to meet someone who could.

Her cell phone rang beside her, and

she checked the name before answering. "Shelby, where in Greece are you now?"

"Actually, we're flying back home in about an hour."

Mel sat up straighter and clutched the phone to her ear, hoping she'd heard that right. "I thought you were planning on staying for another week at least."

"I missed being home." Shelby laughed on the other end. "All these years I've wanted to travel the world, and I discovered that I like being home too."

"That just means you can start planning your next trip."

"Sounds good to me. I'm thinking Paris."

Mel whistled. "Oui."

"Oui, oui." Shelby paused. "How are things with Jack?"

"No offense, Shel, but I don't want to talk about him. Or the men I've been meeting on these dates."

"Wait. Men, as in plural? Good for you."

"Don't get too excited. There have been a lot of first dates, but no seconds." She hadn't even been tempted to see anyone for another date. Her plans for marriage seemed to be further away with dating than they'd been when she'd been staying home. "Maybe I'm not meant to be with someone."

"Oh, please. Of the two of us, you're the one most likely to have a dozen kids and an adoring husband."

"Josh doesn't adore you?"

Shelby giggled on the other end. "Okay, he does. He's the most amazing man I've ever known. One night in Athens, he arranged for a private dinner at this villa that overlooked the sea. It was the most romantic night I've ever had." She sighed, and Mel felt a fleeting moment of jealousy.

"We can discuss your marital bliss after we figure out why I'm not having any luck with this dating strategy."

"I tell you what. Let's meet at my condo for dinner Friday night. I can tell you about our trip, and we can make a game plan for finding you a husband."

"Deal."

Mel hung up the phone and gave the dog a pat on his head. "You don't happen to have any ideas about how to find a husband, do you?"

The dog looked at her, then rested his head on her knee with a sigh. She gave him a scratch behind the ears. "My thoughts exactly."

THE PLANNING MEETING with the committee on Wednesday left Jack with a bad taste in his mouth. Mel showed up in a thin blouse that would do nothing to keep her warm during winter and a skirt with a hem that ensured her legs would be freezing. "Who are you and what have you done with my best friend?" he'd asked, but Mel hadn't answered except to shoot him a nasty look.

So maybe he hadn't handled that right, but who could blame him? His best friend seemed to have changed completely. Mel didn't wear cutesy clothes or shoes that had a heel. She dressed for comfort, not style.

But not anymore.

Once they finished for the evening, Jack was glad to see Mel hang back. Maybe she wanted to be friends again. He'd tell her he missed her. That he couldn't be happy without her. He was about to say as much when she asked, "Have you found the dog's owners yet?"

"The dog? You haven't even given him a name?"

"I'm not keeping him, so no, I haven't named him. What would be the point?"

Jack shook his head. "He's not microchipped, so that was a dead end. And the usual lost pet websites don't have him listed. But I haven't given up on him."

Mel paused and looked down at the table. "What if you don't find his owners?"

"He might have found you instead."

Mel held up a hand. "Like I said, my lifestyle isn't good for a dog. Doggy daycare is okay as a temporary thing, but he doesn't deserve to be in one place all day when I'm working."

"We could figure out an arrangement between the two of us, like a joint custody thing."

"I don't want a dog, so you can have full custody of him."

Jack watched as she put on her coat. He reached out to smooth the lapel and looked into her eyes. "You might change your mind."

She didn't answer him.

"I haven't given up on you either," he murmured, not sure she'd heard him.

Turning on her heel, she left the library and left him wondering when they would have another chance to have that talk.

ON FRIDAY NIGHT after work, Jack shifted the bottle of wine he'd brought with him to his other arm and pressed the doorbell. No answer, so he knocked. He was about to knock again when Josh answered. Jack checked the address again. No, it was Shelby's condo all right. "Is Shelby here?"

"Of course she is. Come in."

Shelby exited the kitchen, adjusting her top as she did so. "Jack, you're early."

He thrust the bottle at her and narrowed his eyes as he observed her swollen lips and smeared lipstick. He turned back to look at Josh whose cheeks colored. "Did I interrupt something?"

Shelby glanced at the wine label. "I'll open this and let it breathe before I serve it. Do lamb chops sound good for dinner?"

"Since when do you eat lamb?"

"Since Greece. Oh, Jack, the food was amazing. You'd have loved it."

"Tell him about that baking lesson we had in Athens."

"And all the ouzo we drank." She put a hand to her chest. "Made me do things I never imagined, let me tell you."

"Remember the scene on the balcony? You professed your love for me to the entire city of Milos."

Shelby burst out laughing and slapped at him. "Don't tell all my secrets."

Jack looked between her and Josh. "I feel like I'm missing something. What happened between you two in Greece? We all knew you were dating, but there's something different about you two now."

Shelby shook her head. "It's called love. You should try it sometime."

The doorbell rang, and Josh walked over to answer it. Jack watched him greet Mel who wore a different dress, this time in a shade of golden brown that matched her eyes. And she'd done something with her hair that made it shine brighter. He swallowed at the sight of her, reminding himself that this was still Mel. His best friend.

Mel looked down at the wrapped gift in her hands and frowned. "I didn't know you were coming tonight."

"This is the first I knew you were invited."

Mel pointed behind her at the door. "Maybe I should go then."

"Stop. Both of you." Shelby looked between them. "You're putting aside all the tension between you two for tonight. The four of us are going to have a pleasant meal, and we're going to catch up on what's been happening, and there's to be no hostility. Do you hear me?"

Mel nodded as Jack rolled his eyes. "Fine. I'll be right back. I want to wash my hands."

He walked down the hall to his cousin's bathroom and shut the door behind him. He turned the water on and pumped some soap into his hands, massaging them to produce a lather. And saw two toothbrushes sitting in the cup beside the faucet. He rinsed off his hands, then opened the medicine cabinet. A man's razor and shaving cream next to Shelby's toiletries. What in the world was going on here? Since when did Josh leave his things at Shelby's condo?

He returned from the bathroom and stared at Josh. "You've got some kind of nerve, buster."

"Excuse me?"

"Shelby's always had a good head on her shoulders, but you show up and all of a sudden she's throwing her good sense out the window."

"What are you talking about?"

Jack turned to Shelby and pointed at Josh. "Is he living here with you?"

"Yes, but don't get that look on your face. It's not what you think."

"You've only been dating for three months, and he just moves in without a serious discussion of what you're doing to your future?"

"I am thinking of my future, and it's with Josh. That's what you're supposed to do when you get married, isn't it?"

She covered her mouth as Josh crossed the room to put his arm around her and faced Jack. "We eloped in Greece. But you can't tell anyone in the family yet."

"They're going to find out eventually."

Unfortunately, gossip had a tendency to get around the family pretty quick. Half of them seemed to know he was getting divorced before his wife had told him. "You need to tell them. Soon."

Shelby nodded. "And I will tell them. But first, we're trying to figure out where we're going to live. We have Josh's dad to think about now, and my apartment is too small for the three of us."

Jack glanced at Mel. "Did you know about this?"

Mel nodded and handed the gift to Shelby. "Congratulations to you both." She kissed first Shelby on the cheek, then Josh, before turning to Jack. "Isn't that what you wanted to say to them?"

He didn't know what to say. He liked Josh. But that didn't change the fact that they barely knew each other. "I just need a minute to get over the shock. I mean, you guys got married? Isn't that awfully quick?"

"Well, I think it's romantic." Mel turned to Shelby. "I want to hear all the details. Where was it? What did you wear? Did you write your own vows?"

Shelby embraced her friend and pulled her into the kitchen, talking a mile a minute. Jack glanced at Josh, then held out a hand. "Welcome to the family, and good luck. You're going to need it."

"Her parents thought our relationship was moving too fast when they found out we were traveling to Greece together. I can't imagine what they'll say when they find out we got married without them present."

"Some words of advice? Her dad's a traditionalist, so you might think about asking for his blessing. Even if it is after the fact."

They shook hands. "And her mother?"

"Tell her that you'll have another ceremony here, with all the bells and whistles. She'll be so happy planning the wedding reception to be upset much."

"If only it were that easy."

Jack nodded, knowing Josh had a long road ahead of him.

ONCE DINNER HAD been eaten, the four of them settled in the living room as Shelby and Josh took turns telling stories about their trip, sipping the wine Jack had brought with him. Mel stole a glance at him over the rim of her glass. He looked good. Almost too good as he lounged on the other end of the sofa, laughing at Shelby's story about being attacked by hungry seagulls on a Grecian beach.

"I was trying to feed the one who wasn't getting any from the other tourists, not the whole flock."

Josh smiled and pulled her into the crook of his arm. "That's my wife. Always thinking about the one not getting their fair share." He shook his head. "My wife. Wow. That's going to take some getting used to."

"What does your dad think about all this?" Mel asked, knowing that Josh had been taking care of Bert after Josh's mom died last year. "Are you moving him in here too?"

Josh and Shelby exchanged looks, and he shrugged. "We talked about it, but it would be pretty tight quarters with him here. We'll start looking for a house that will fit all of us and move in the New Year. Until then, I'll still be keeping my eye on him. And so will Shelby. But he agrees that we need some privacy in the beginning since we're newlyweds."

Mel looked again over at Jack who seemed to agree with that, nodding with Josh's words. Why did he have to show up here tonight wearing that blue sweater that brought out the same color in his eyes? She'd bought him the sweater for Christmas two years ago, and she always liked it when he wore it.

But she was over him. Sort of. She was going out on dates with other men. She'd gotten a makeover to prove that she was moving on from Jack.

So why did it feel as if she were in the same exact place that she'd been only two weeks before? Why did she still wonder what he thought about her? Ask herself if he liked her outfit? And why did she miss him at night so much that she picked up her phone to call him only to put it back down and cry?

Mel noticed that everyone's eyes were on her and realized that she'd missed something. Shelby smirked as if she knew where her thoughts had been. "I was asking how the planning was going for the fundraiser."

Oh. "Good. Better now that you're home and can take my place on the committee."

Shelby held up her hand. "Before you go down that road, I have to tell you that I'm not taking over my spot again. I'll need you to continue cochairing with Jack until the fundraiser."

"But I agreed to only be on the committee until you returned."

"Which is why I feel bad that I can't do it full-time like I was. I can be on the committee and help out where I can, but I won't be leading things this year."

Mel frowned at her friend, feeling as if she was missing something. "Why can't you? What is so important that you would turn your back on your family's event?"

"I'm not turning my back. I just can't commit full-time." She glanced at Josh. "I'm in the middle of selling the garage to Eddie, then setting up my own accounting office. Plus, there's Great-aunt Sarah's wedding and helping Josh with his dad. It's all too much, and I need to prioritize where I'm needed most. And from what I've heard, Aunt Sarah says you and Jack are doing a great job."

"Fine. I get it. You're too busy. I guess I'll have to stick it out."

"Is working with me that difficult?" Jack asked her, and she turned to find that he'd sat up and stared at her. "I thought things were going okay."

"Of course you did. You figured that I'd be the same old reliable Mel who would drop everything to help you out. But I'm in the middle of trying to get my own life figured out too, you know."

He shrugged. "Maybe if you stopped worrying about your appearance, which was nice before, by the way, and focused on who your friends are, you'd see that I want to be a part of your life too. I don't appreciate being ignored."

"Jack…" Shelby's mouth dropped open. "I can't believe you'd say something like that."

Mel stood, shaking her head. She turned to Jack who had also risen to his feet. "You keep talking about how you still want to be friends, but you don't say things like that to someone who is a friend." She gave a short nod to Shelby and Josh. "I hope you don't mind if I leave early. I have to open the store by myself in the morning."

"Mel, you don't have to leave." Shelby glared at Jack before following her to the front door where she grabbed her coat. "We haven't even had dessert yet."

"I'm not very hungry." Mel squeezed Shelby in a tight hug. "Thank you for the delicious dinner and sharing all your stories. I'm so happy for you and Josh. I really am."

Shelby glanced at Josh who came up to them. "Please don't go, Melanie."

She looked over his shoulder to where Jack stood, staring out the window. Now he couldn't even look at her? She took a deep breath to get a handle on her emotions. She could cry in the car on her way home if she needed to. Instead, she pasted a smile on her face. Why was protecting her heart considered selfish? "The three of us should get together again soon."

She gripped her purse and shot another look at Jack before walking out the front door.

SHELBY STORMED OVER to Jack and pointed to the front door. "Go and get her back here, Jack, or I swear we're not cousins anymore."

"I can't."

"Can't or won't?"

Jack hadn't meant to say what he'd said to Mel. Would never have believed that he would say anything so mean about his best friend. What was worse, he didn't know how to make the situation right. "How?"

"This is Mel. You know how to fix this."

"Not this Mel. She's someone I don't even recognize anymore."

"That doesn't give you an excuse for saying what you did. You were raised better than that. So you go and apologize to her right now."

Jack looked at his cousin and knew she was right. He closed his eyes for a moment, then ran out the front door calling Mel's name. She had gotten to her car and was already inside when he reached it, standing behind it so that she wouldn't be able to leave without running him over.

Which she might be thinking about doing. Maybe blocking her in wasn't a great idea.

Her driver's side window rolled down,

and she stuck her head out of it. "Get out of the way, Jack. I'm going home."

"Not until you hear what I have to say."

"I've heard plenty from you tonight. Now move." She stuck her head back inside and put the car into Reverse.

Jack kept his position until the rear bumper rested against his thigh. "I'm sorry, Mel. I shouldn't have said what I did."

Her head poked out of the window again, then she put the car in Park and climbed out, the door wide open, the engine still idling. She stood a few feet away from him. "Then why did you?"

"Because I'm an idiot."

"Yes, you are."

"And I don't know if this new version is the best version of you."

Mel held her arms out to her sides. "What's so wrong with me getting a haircut and buying some new clothes? I'm still the same me that I've always been."

"But are you still my best friend?" He took a step closer to her, and she backed away at his approach. He gave a nod as if that was the answer he'd expected. "Because I really miss her. I miss talking to her about the weird or unexpected things that happened during my day. Miss spending time with her even if we're sitting and doing nothing but watching our favorite TV show. I don't know about this new you."

"No, you knew the version of me that was safe. That was firmly in the friend zone and therefore nonthreatening."

"I was never threatened by you."

"Really? Then this should be just fine for you."

She stepped forward and kissed him. This kiss was different than the last time she'd kissed him. There was no question on her end. But it raised only more in his mind.

He put his hands up to her face, then leaned away from her. "Don't do this, Mel."

"This is what I want. And neither of us can help how we feel." She stepped away. "I want more than friendship from you, Jack. It's why I think you need to start looking for a new best friend because I can't do this anymore."

She got into her car, and he moved aside to let her leave.

He returned to Shelby's condo alone. Shelby looked behind him. "Where is she?" She shook her head at him. "You're going to lose her, Jack."

That was the problem. "I already have."

"Is that what you really want?"

No. It was the exact opposite. By now, Mel should know that he needed her. Maybe not in the way she wanted, but their relationship was one of the most important in his life. "Why can't she just accept that we're friends and nothing more?"

"Because the two of you have always been more than that."

"I don't have those kinds of feelings for her."

"Really? Because it's pretty obvious to everybody else that you do and always have."

He scowled. "Then you're all wrong. I'm not in love with her and never will be."

Shelby reached over and took his hand. "Jack, you're a man of science. You come up with a theory, then test it through observations and gathering data. Don't you think it's time you test our theory that you're just as in love with Mel as she is with you?"

CHAPTER FIVE

SHELBY'S THEORY THAT Jack was in love with Mel was just that—a theory. Even if it was seriously flawed and completely false. But maybe Shelby was right about one thing. It was past time that he gathered data about his own theory on his relationships. Because while he might be great at friendship, he seemed to be doomed to fail in romance. His dating history had proven that. And if he could figure out what went wrong in the past, then he might be able to change things so that he could find a love that lasted in the future.

One of his failed relationships, Ashley, had agreed to meet him that Saturday afternoon at the cider mill. He parked in the crowded lot, then followed the wooden signs past the corn maze and the pumpkin patch to find her watching for him in front of a large barn. She smiled at his approach, and he thought maybe this wouldn't be so bad after all. Maybe they still had something of a spark left there.

"I was shocked to get your call," she told him after giving him a brief hug.

"I was surprised you answered it." He remembered her telling him to never call her again when they'd broken up almost a year before. But he'd convinced her that he wasn't interested in dating again this time. Just wanted to talk. But maybe if things worked out, they could pick up where they had left off.

She shrugged. "Enough time has passed that I figured I could talk to you without plotting your demise."

Ouch. Jack winced at her words. Then again, maybe they didn't have anything but hard feelings left between them. He led her into the barn where they purchased a half gallon of cider and a dozen fresh donuts still warm from frying in oil and dusted with cinnamon sugar. Once he paid for their treat, they stepped outside and located a glass-topped bistro table with two wrought iron chairs. Ashley took one of the chairs and opened the cider, pouring them both a plastic cupful as Jack took the other chair and placed a couple donuts on top of a napkin in front of each of them. They ate donuts and drank in silence for a moment. After finishing his second donut, Jack asked, "Were things really that bad between us?"

Ashley paused and shook her head. "No, things weren't bad. But do you know how many dates you stood me up for? We only dated for three months, and you canceled on me five times."

That couldn't be right. "I'm sure it wasn't that many."

"And then you left me during the middle of our dates twice."

That he did remember. One time had been for doing emergency surgery on a Persian cat that had been in a nasty fight with a Doberman pinscher. The other had been to remove a number of magnetic balls from the stomach of a black Labrador. "The clinic is very demanding on my time. I'm on call twenty-four hours a day. I thought that was clear when we started dating."

Ashley folded her hands on the table

and looked across at him. "That's what you told me every single time you canceled on me, but I didn't quite believe you actually meant twenty-four seven."

"But it was true. And it still is." He glanced at his phone which had buzzed. Just a text from his mother confirming dinner the following night. He looked up to find Ashley staring at him. "Did you expect me to put sick or injured animals on hold because I was attempting to have a social life?"

Ashley put her hand up to stop whatever he was going to say next. "I expected to be seen as a priority at least once in a while. But I didn't even make the top three on your list."

"What are you talking about? What three?"

She counted them off on her fingers. "Your job. Your family. And then there was Melanie."

Jack frowned at her words. "What does Mel have to do with this?" And why did everyone seem to bring her up with him? Why could no one seem to accept that he and Mel were just friends and always would be?

"If you don't know about how she came between us, then I'm not telling you. You're oblivious when it comes to her." She glanced at her watch. "Listen. This walk down memory lane has been…interesting and the donuts were great, but I've got to go."

When he'd called and made plans with her, they'd talked about getting together and maybe having dinner afterward. But they hadn't been together more than twenty minutes. "I thought we were meeting so that we could catch up with each other."

"And we just did. Talking to you now has just reminded me why I broke up with you in the first place. And your phone just buzzed again. I'm sure Mel needs something else from you." She stood, leaned over and kissed his cheek. "Good luck, Jack. I wish you the best."

And then she walked away, leaving him staring after her and wondering what had just happened. This was supposed to be about gathering data on his past relationships, but they hadn't had enough time for him to get all that he needed.

He checked his phone, but there was no message from Mel. He almost wished there had been one. Instead, it was Shelby reminding him that the printer needed the fundraiser information to finalize the posters and tickets. It was the third text in the last twenty-four hours from her regarding details about the event. If she was so worried about it getting done, she should still be in charge of it.

But instead of pointing that out to her, he texted back that he had already confirmed with the printer and would be picking up everything the next Thursday morning.

Jack opened the bag of donuts and took out another, munching on it while he contemplated this meeting with Ashley. He was right about his job coming between them, but it was her assertion that his relationship with Mel had done the same thing. Had he made her a higher priority than the woman he'd been dating? He filtered through his memories, but it didn't seem to match up with his recollection of their relationship. Every single time, it had been his career that had interfered with his relationship with Ashley. She had to be wrong about Mel.

He blew out a puff of air and mentally shook his head as if to clear the information on the screen. Work had always come first and always would. He was dedicated to the animals he cared for.

Thinking of them, he rose to his feet. He had a couple of Himalayan kittens that needed their stitches checked, and now he had a free evening to himself. The thought of another night home alone made him shudder. It really wouldn't hurt to stop in to the clinic for a few minutes.

KRISTINA PURSED HER lips as she took in the outfit that Mel had tried on. Mel looked down at herself, then turned to peer at her figure in the three faceted mirrors in the dressing room to figure out what Kristina's expression meant. "I don't understand. What's wrong with what I'm wearing?"

"Where do you want me to start?"

"You told me to pick something feminine and hinting at my sexuality without flaunting it." Mel fingered the lace overset of the skirt. "This has it all."

"Just because it has lace and flowers doesn't make it feminine. And you're hinting something all right." Kristina turned Mel to look at herself from a different angle in the mirror. "This outfit screams too young to be taken seriously."

She knew Kristina was right as she took in the details that made her look like a preteen trying to dress up in her mother's clothes. Mel groaned. "Why am I so bad at this? I've been reading all these books on fashion to learn, but I can't seem to remember their advice when I'm choosing an outfit. Maybe I should be taking notes or something and bringing them with me on these shopping trips."

"Not everyone is as gifted at this as I am." Kristina pushed her toward the dressing room. "Now try on one of the outfits I chose for you. That one with the ruby top first."

Mel shut the door to the dressing room and changed into the one Kristina had mentioned. When she walked out of the dressing room, she found Shelby standing there holding up a cotton candy–pink dress. "I found this in the sales racks and thought it was perfect for you."

Kristina plucked the garment from her cousin and shook her head. "Not even close. Leave this up to the expert." She took Mel's hand and pulled her to the mirrors. "Now, this is an outfit that says you're a woman who is ready to find a serious relationship. It's sophisticated and looks as if it was tailored for your body."

Mel plucked at the neckline. "You don't think it's a little too revealing? I don't have much here to be flaunting, but it seems awfully low-cut."

Kristina thrust a camisole at her. "Try this on underneath. It will give you more coverage, and I think you'll find that you'll be more comfortable wearing it like that."

Shelby took a seat on the padded bench. "Where did you learn all this stuff?"

"I look at others whose style I admire. I listen to advice and read fashion magazines. And I try to learn from the best. Then I put it all into practice." Kristina pointed to the dressing room. "Now try on the other outfit I picked out for you."

Mel could hear the cousins chatting as she tried on the second outfit, a soft sweater in a dark plum with tailored tan trousers in a size smaller than she normally wore. She departed the dressing room to a whistle from Shelby. "What have you done with my best friend? Very classy and sophisticated."

Mel looked down at herself. "I always wear blouses, sweaters and pants to work at the bookstore. How is this any different?"

"First of all, what you're wearing is in the right size for your body. And second, these are tailored to follow the lines of your body rather than hiding it." Kristina reached over and tugged on the hem of the sweater. "See how the shape of the sweater gives you curves? This is what you should be wearing not just on dates, but to work and to live your best life. Check yourself out. You look amazing."

Mel looked at her reflection and couldn't help but agree. "So should I wear this or the ruby blouse for my date tonight?"

"Where are you going?"

"To hear a friend of his play at a restaurant."

"The ruby. What you're wearing now would be something to wear to meet his family."

Mel fingered the edge of the sweater. "It's our first date. We haven't even talked about a second one, so there's no meeting any family yet."

Shelby smiled. "You just said *yet* like you have some hope about this relationship."

Maybe she did have a little pinch of hope when it came to Marius. Whenever she thought about him, she got a nervous feeling in her belly like she was about to start something that could change her life. "I'm not saying that I'm in love with Marius or anything, but he's a nice guy with some potential at this point."

"And are you meeting him at the restaurant tonight?" Kristina pursed her lips as she waited for the answer.

Mel shook her head. "No, he's picking me up at my house."

"Finally, you're listening to me. This date has some great potential already."

Or it would have potential if he ever showed up, Mel thought later as she checked out the front window to the street to catch a glimpse of his car. She checked the time on her phone again. Twenty minutes after when they'd agreed to meet, and no text or call to say he was running behind. She'd give him ten more minutes, then she'd call. Maybe they'd agreed to meet at seven thirty and not seven?

She resisted the urge to keep staring out the window and walked to her sofa and took a seat, clasping her hands in front of her to keep from calling him. Her phone chimed with a text message alert, and she held her breath as she looked at the screen. Not Marius, but Jack had texted her.

I shouldn't have said what I did last night. Forgive me?

She closed her eyes and counted to five. The urge to text him back was too strong, and she refrained from rushing to respond to him. Let him sweat it a little. In fact, let him stew a lot because she didn't know how to respond to that. His words had hurt her, but his rebuff at her kiss had wounded her even more. She would have to try to accept the situation for what it was, but so should he.

Her phone chimed again. Please. I hate when we fight.

Well, she did too. But that didn't mean she should reply to him so quickly. She wished Marius had picked her up when agreed; she'd be enjoying her date with a man who wanted to be with her and would treat her with respect. It might even be an evening that would end with a kiss.

The knock on the front door took her attention off the phone. Marius had finally arrived. The dog ran to the door, barking. Mel answered it to find Jack instead of Marius standing there on her porch. "Hey. Can I come in?"

"What are you doing here?"

"I wanted to apologize in person."

She looked out the door to see his car parked outside. "Were you texting me from the driveway?"

He gave a shrug and a crooked smile, and she knew at that moment she would forgive him because he was her best friend and that's what best friends did. She stepped aside so that he could enter the house. When she shut the door and turned to face him, he looked down at what she was wearing. "You're going on a date, aren't you? I knew I should have called ahead."

"Don't worry. He's running late." She crossed her arms over her chest. "Now what was this you were saying about apologizing to me?"

Jack knelt down to give the dog a belly rub. "Not letting me off the hook, are you?"

"Why should I?"

He stood and ran a hand through his hair, mussing it in the way that made him look like he had in high school. She longed to reach up and straighten it, but clenched her fists to resist the temptation.

Jack peered at her. "I don't want to lose our friendship because that means more to me than almost anything else in the entire world."

"Almost?"

He gave a shrug. "Well, there's my clinic and my family, of course. But you're right up there." He took a step toward her. "I know that I'm messing up things between us because I'm having a hard time dealing with this new version of you. For that, I am genuinely sorry. But your shutting me out is painful for the both of us. And I don't want to hurt anymore. Do you?"

She looked into his bright blue eyes and knew that he was speaking his truth. It might not be what she wanted to hear, but he had shared what was in his heart. Just like she had shared what was in hers on Halloween. She turned away from him to try to get her feelings under control. Blinking quickly to keep the tears from falling, she took several deep breaths before turning back to him. "I don't want to hurt anymore either, Jack. That's why I said what I did."

"I'm still confused. Why does it have to be all or nothing with this?"

"Can you be friends with me if I'm dating other men?"

He took her hand in his and held it against his chest. "We have in the past. Why can't we again? What has changed?"

It would be so easy to let things go back to what they had been. And she'd end up hurting because he could never give her what she wanted. She couldn't do that again. Wouldn't do that.

But what if this time she finally gave up the dream of a future with Jack and focused instead on finding a man who loved her back? She could be strong enough to release this unrequited love for the man in front of her. Concentrate instead on nurturing a relationship with someone who wanted to be her partner.

Thinking of Marius, she took her hand from Jack's hold and glanced at her phone and frowned. "He hasn't called or texted."

"Who?"

She tapped out a quick text to Marius asking if she had the time wrong. "My date."

"How late is he?"

"Twenty-seven minutes. But who's counting?"

Jack took a step closer to her. "Mel, what about us? Are we okay now?"

She looked up at him and gave him a nod. "You're right. We should still be friends. I don't want to lose years of friendship over this."

He sighed and gave her a quick hug. "Good. Because I've missed you. I want to hear all your news. And I have so much to tell you too."

"Well, you might as well take a seat on the sofa because that could take a while."

Jack laughed. "Fair enough." He glanced behind her at the dog who had returned to his post on the sofa. "You look right at home there, buddy." Jack walked over and took a seat next to the dog.

Mel put a hand on the dog's head. "Don't get too used to it, mister. Jack is still trying to find you an owner." She looked up at him with a sinking suspicion. "You are still looking, right?"

He held up two fingers. "I honestly am, but I think our search for his old owners is pointless. It's time to try finding him a new family."

He nodded at her. "And if we're being honest with each other, I do think you look really nice with the hair and the makeup and everything."

She smiled, then checked her phone again. Still no text. Nothing. Not a word from Marius. "Should I call him? See if I had the wrong time or something?" She looked at Jack. "What would you do in this situation?"

"I wouldn't be late, for one thing."

"Oh, please. You canceled on your girl-friends all the time."

"But I always let them know beforehand. I didn't let them sit and stew wondering where I was."

"I'm not stewing." He raised his eye-brows at that, but she wouldn't let that stop her from contemplating where Marius might be. "You know what? I'm call-ing him."

She dialed his number and waited as it rang five times before going to voicemail. "Hey, Marius. It's Melanie. I must have gotten the wrong time or maybe the wrong day for our date. Can you call me back when you get this message? Thanks."

When she hung up the phone, she found Jack watching her. "You're letting him off the hook? Just like that?"

She frowned and glanced at her phone. "I am not."

"You put the blame on yourself. Said that maybe you got the wrong time or day.

Not that it was his fault that he was late or standing you up."

She bristled at the suggestion. "He's not standing me up."

Jack cocked his head to one side to look at her. "Is this your first date with this guy?"

"They've all been first dates." She covered her face with her hands. "Is there something so wrong with me that I can't find a decent guy interested in me?"

Jack put his arms around her shoulders and pulled her close to him. "You're perfect. It's the guys who are idiots."

She rested her cheek on his shoulder, reveling in the feel of his hard chest against her. "Still feels like it's my fault. I feel so single. I'm probably destined to be alone."

"You just haven't found the right one yet."

She lifted her head to look into his eyes. "And what if I never find him?"

Jack reached up and pushed back a strand of her hair that had fallen over one eye. "You will."

"I wish I could believe you."

He smiled at her, and she wished he was

right. Jack led Mel to the sofa and sat next to her, the dog lying between them. "How about I stay with you for a while?"

"He might still show up."

"Then I'll leave when he gets here. Or better yet, I'll watch the dog while you go out." He reached for the remote and turned on the television. "In the meantime, we can watch our show while we wait. Or have you been watching without me?"

Mel put a hand to her chest and dropped open her mouth. "Would I do that?"

He queued up the next episode of the series they'd been watching before their argument and let it start playing. "You've been watching ahead of me all season, then pretending that you haven't seen it yet. Admit it."

"I admit nothing." But she couldn't help but smile.

AFTER A FEW episodes of their show, it became obvious that this guy wasn't showing up. Jack could have told her that when he'd arrived. If the guy wanted to be with her, he would have arrived on time or at least called to say he was running late. That's what he would have done. He wouldn't make Melanie wait without a word from him.

At the end of the current episode, he stood and stretched. "I'm starving. Want to order a pizza or something?"

Mel pulled out her phone and stared at the empty screen. "He's not coming, is he?"

Jack sat next to her and put a hand on her knee as she started to tear up. "Hey. This is not on you. It's on him, okay? He's the jerk for not being here and not calling you to let you know."

"I thought he was going to be different than the others." She took a deep breath, then opened an app on the phone. "You want your usual meat lovers pizza?"

"You know I do."

As she ordered their dinner, he retrieved plates and napkins from her kitchen and placed them on the coffee table in front of the sofa. A second trip produced cans of pop which he carefully placed on top of coasters. He'd learned his lesson the last time that he'd forgotten to use one.

While they waited for their pizza, they

started another episode, but Jack paused it five minutes into the show when he noticed that Mel wasn't paying attention. She looked over at him. "Why did you stop it?"

"Because you're not watching. You'd rather talk about this guy and how he's hurt you."

She shook her head. "He doesn't seem like the kind of guy who would stand me up. Now I'm worried that something might have happened to him."

He looked at her, noting the downturn of her lips and the droop at the edges of her golden brown eyes. "What you said earlier, about there being something wrong with you?" He shook his head. "There's nothing I would change about you. You're perfect."

She gave a snort. "Please. I haven't dated anyone seriously since Tom. And he turned out to be a major jerk."

Jack bit his tongue from calling the guy something stronger than *jerk*. The man had played with her heart and cheated on her more times than he had fingers. "But that doesn't mean there's something wrong with you."

"I wish I could believe that."

Jack nudged her forward and wrapped his arms around her. "Well, believe it. And that's your best friend who loves you more than anything saying that."

He continued to hold her, trying to ignore the warmth of her breath on his shoulder or the way that she fit perfectly against him. He closed his eyes for a moment, but opened them when her phone buzzed. She let him go and grabbed her phone. She read the text and nodded before texting the sender back. "That was Marius. He's had a family emergency, so he can't make our date tonight. I'm so relieved."

"See? I told you. There's nothing wrong with you."

She smiled, then leaned forward and pecked him on the lips. The doorbell rang, and she got up to get their dinner while Jack remained sitting on the sofa, wondering why he had a sudden urge to hold her and kiss her a little longer.

WHILE THEY ATE DINNER, they watched another episode of their show, leaning back into the sofa cushions, their plates resting on their full bellies. Mel looked over at Jack when he laughed at something a character said and took in the hard planes of his face. He was so handsome, but he didn't see that. To her, he was the best-looking guy in the world. And don't think she didn't notice how he slipped the dog pieces of pizza crust when he thought she wasn't looking.

He turned to find her staring at him, and she sat up quickly, grabbing her plate before it slid off her stomach and onto the floor. "I just had a great idea. We should sign you up for the dating app that I'm on. I'm sure you could find a girlfriend on there, no problem."

"Finding a girlfriend isn't the problem. Keeping her is." But he too sat up and placed his empty plate on the coffee table.

She grabbed his phone from the sofa where it lay between them and entered his password. He nudged her in the side with his elbow. "Since when do you have my pass code?"

"Oh, please. You always pick the most obvious numbers."

"I didn't choose my birthday."

"No, you used mine." She turned and

grinned at him. "You also use it for your PIN and your alarm code at the clinic. And, I'm just guessing here, but also your laptop?"

"Stop being so smug."

She returned her gaze to his phone and downloaded the app. "I've been studying plenty of articles and books on how to create the best profile to get the most interest from potential dates, so I'll start it off for you." She entered his name, email and then the basic physical characteristics. Five foot eleven. Built. Blue eyes and sandy brown hair. She added the detail about his short beard, but hoped he'd shave it off soon. "What do you want in a relationship?" Mel turned to him, then started typing, *I'm looking for companionship and affection, someone who can be my best friend.*

He peered over her shoulder and watched as she typed. "How do you know all this stuff about me?"

"Hello? Best friend for twenty-five years? I think anyone would say that I have you down pat."

"Hmm, we'll see."

She held out the phone to him. "You want to change it?"

He looked at her for a moment, then shook his head. "No, you're right. I am looking for someone who can be a friend and a lover."

She swallowed at the heat in her cheeks as he said those words. *Focus on Jack's profile*, she reminded herself. "Okay, describe your perfect date."

"April twenty-fifth."

She grinned at his movie reference. "Haha, but seriously. What would a perfect date with you be like?"

"Having dinner, since I obviously need food. And then I don't know…" He looked off into the distance.

"Going to see a superhero movie," Mel said as she typed it in. "Followed by dessert and conversation." She looked up at him. "Sound about right?"

He nodded. "Okay, since you know me so well, what about the next question? What is a turnoff?"

She knew the answer to that one without having to think too hard. Jack couldn't stand a woman who was cruel to people and especially animals. She typed the answer in and held the phone out for him to see. He gave a nod. "True."

"Turn-ons?"

He leaned back and held out a hand as if to let her answer the question. The problem with this one was she didn't know. If she did, they might already be dating now. Deciding to wing it, she typed, *Intelligence. Sense of humor. Compassion.*

Jack groaned as he read it. "You're right about that, but you make me sound like I'm all touchy-feely with those words."

"Then what would you write?"

He took the phone and erased what she had written and replaced it with *Attractive inside and out. Can make me laugh.*

"How is that different from what I wrote?"

"It just is."

"The books say to be specific, and right now we're being too broad. What's one precise detail that you would say turns you on?"

His cheeks brightened, and he turned away to type something into the phone. Mel tried to peek around him, but he kept hunching over so that she couldn't see it. When he finished, he turned the phone for her to read. *Loves to read spy thrillers with a female protagonist and discuss them.*

"A female protagonist?"

He gave a shrug. "You know they're my favorite. Besides, it makes me sound sensitive."

"But you are sensitive."

"Well-rounded then."

They worked on his profile for the next twenty minutes, then submitted it to the app. Jack frowned when no matches came up. "Not even one woman who is close enough to what I want?"

"This app doesn't give you immediate results because it goes deeper than the other ones do. You'll probably get a few notifications in the next day or so just like I did."

"But your matches haven't worked out."

She frowned at this. They really hadn't. "Okay, then maybe you can help me fix what I have on my profile. Maybe I can attract a better candidate that way." She grabbed her phone, logged into the app and pressed the edit button to access her profile.

"Read me what you have."

"'Bookworm looking for her prince in disguise.'"

Jack made a noise at the back of his throat and stared at her. "And that's gotten you dates?"

"I'm not finished reading it." She turned back to her phone. "'Looking for a man who loves books and hates how they're portrayed in the movies. Someone who enjoys nights out on the town as well as quiet evenings at home. Can this beauty turn your beast into a prince?'"

"And this is what the books recommended that you put in your profile?"

"Not exactly." To be honest, she hadn't liked the advice the books had given her. "I used some of what they said, then went off in my own direction."

Jack shook his head and leaned over to press the edit button. "First of all, most guys are basing their decision to get to know you on your profile picture. Not any description that you've come up with." He gave her a look when he looked up from the phone. "This is the best picture you had?"

"There's nothing wrong with the picture." She had taken a selfie wearing one of the outfits that Kristina had recommended. And she'd done her hair and makeup just the way she liked. She thought she looked pretty good, if she said so herself.

Jack grabbed his phone and started scrolling through his photos until he chose one and held it up for her to see. "This is my favorite picture of you. This is the one you should use."

In it, she had been laughing hard at something he had said. He'd caught her midlaugh, head tipped back, eyes closed. "Why? You can't get a good idea of what I look like."

"Because this is the real you." He stared down at the picture. "This is the woman who I would want to get to know better." He looked up at her. "She's intriguing. I'd want to find out what made her laugh like that. What brought her joy so contagious that I find myself wanting it too."

Mel reached for his phone and studied

her picture. "You got all that from this image?"

"I told you. It's my favorite picture of you."

"Well, I don't look anything like that now." That picture was from before she'd told Jack how she felt. Before her makeover. "And you're saying that this woman is more attractive to you than..." She glanced around the room and picked up a nearby magazine and flipped pages until she found a model draped over a statue of an ancient goddess. She pointed her finger to the woman. "More attractive than her?"

He looked at her and nodded slowly. "I would much rather be in a relationship with you than with this model."

Mel looked into his eyes, and she could see the truth shining out of them. "Then I don't understand. If I'm so perfect, why don't you love me?"

"The thing is that I do love you. I love that you're a strong, intelligent woman who turns to books when things don't go according to plan. I love that you spend five minutes going over a menu because you want to try something new but can't decide what it is, then end up ordering the same thing you always get. I love that you've been by my side through everything. All the ups and downs. I've already told you that I can't imagine my life without you. You're an amazing friend."

"But you're not in love with me."

"If I could change that, I would." He shook his head "But that doesn't mean there's something wrong with you. Like I said, you're perfect. And all these guys are dumb if they can't see what I do."

Mel pulled him into a hug. It was exactly what she had needed to hear. "Thank you for saying that."

"I mean it. Every word." He rubbed her back as she rested her cheek on his shoulder. "Someday soon you're going to meet a great guy who thinks you're just as wonderful as I do."

She only hoped that it was soon enough to make her forget her feelings for Jack.

JACK PLACED HIS baby nephew on his shoulder and started to pat his back, hoping that the kid would burp without leaving a trail of milk on his shirt. "Come on, man. We're the only boys in the last two generations within the family. Help a guy out, huh?"

His nephew belched without spitting up, and Jack gave the baby a fist bump after cradling him in his arms. "Thanks, Gavin."

Jack's sister, Michele, took her son from him. "I saw Melanie at the grocery store the other day. She's looking great, isn't she? The new haircut? And those clothes she's wearing? Kristina mentioned that she was giving her a hand, but I'd say that the woman has got it going on. And it's about time too. I've always said that she was a knockout deep down."

He gave a nod, but didn't say a word. Not sure how to respond. He'd always thought that Melanie was cute, but lately he'd found her appealing to the point that he was having difficulty not thinking about her. Maybe it wasn't an issue. He was merely observing like the scientist that he was.

"Do you know if she's seeing anyone?"

No, thank goodness.

He frowned at the thought. He didn't want Mel to be alone anymore, but maybe he was a little worried that a new man in her life might squeeze him out of it. "No one serious."

Michele crossed the living room to hand the baby to her husband. "What do you think about setting her up with your friend Jefferson? He's single too, right?"

Colin shook his head as he settled the baby against his chest. "No more match-making, Michele. Let's leave that to your aunt Sarah."

"What about Sam and Molly? That was my idea."

Colin shook his head again. "They broke up after two dates."

"Okay. Then what about Lara and Nick?"

Jack held up a finger. "She broke off the engagement. Everyone in town was there to witness that at the Fall Festival."

"But at least they got to an engagement." Michele paused, then smiled as if she'd figured it out. "Christopher and Penny."

Her husband laughed as Jack told her, "That was all Great-aunt Sarah. You don't get credit for that one. Sorry."

Michele pouted and took a seat next to Colin. "Fine. But I think Melanie would be a good fit for Jefferson. Why don't you ask her if she'd be interested, Jack?"

"She's getting enough dates on her own, but I'll let her know you have someone in mind."

Michele peered at him. "Do you have a problem with her going out with these guys?"

"Why would I have a problem? She's single. They're single."

"And so are you. Unless the rumors about you and Ashley getting back together are true."

Their meetup had just happened the day before. How had Michele already gotten wind of it? "Nothing's going on between Ashley and me. It was just a matter of finding closure on that relationship. It lasted all of twenty minutes."

"And you and Mel?"

"I've told you before. Melanie and I are just friends."

Colin nudged Michele. "Leave the guy alone, will you?"

Jack nodded at his brother-in-law, appreciating the backup, then looked around the living room. Sunday dinners with his family were a given, especially for his father, who'd finally retired from the police force. "Where's Dad?"

"He's working on something in the garage," his mom answered as she entered the room, wiping her hands on a kitchen towel. She glanced at the grandfather clock that had been a staple in their living room since before Jack had been born. "Can you go tell him there's about fifteen more minutes before the lasagna is finished? And he needs to wash his hands before we eat."

Jack had been hoping to talk alone with his dad, so he nodded at her, then got up from the lounger and walked through the kitchen to the door that led to the attached garage. His dad looked up from the table saw as Jack entered. "Your mother send you to tell me dinner is ready?"

"Fifteen more minutes." He glanced at the workbench that ran along the back of the garage. "What are you working on?"

His dad started to sand the piece of wood he'd just cut. "Something for your mother for Christmas." They stood in silence, the only sound the scraping of sandpaper against wood. His father looked up at him. "Is there something you want to talk about?"

"Yes, sir." Jack took a deep breath and ran a hand through his short hair. "I've been thinking about your job when I was growing up." His dad had been a policeman who eventually became the chief of police in Thora. He'd worked many nights and holidays, missing Little League games and school events. Now that he was retired, he spent more time with family, but Jack had resented the times his dad had been absent when he was growing up. "How did you and Mom make your marriage work when you were always at the police station?"

His dad stopped sanding and looked over at him, letting out a puff of air. "Good question. Not one I'm sure I know the answer to off the top of my head."

"You and Mom are still together, so you obviously did something right."

His dad considered this and shook his head. "It was all your mom. She made a lot of compromises as I made it up the ladder to chief. Took a lot on her shoulders because I couldn't always be there." He paused, then took a step toward Jack. "I don't regret being police chief, but I missed out on a lot of things with you and your sister. Maybe we might have been closer if I had been around more during the time you were growing up."

"We're fine, Dad." True, he might wish they were closer too, but they still had a good relationship. Better than they'd had when he'd been a teenager. "Things are okay with us."

"I'm at the stage of life where I look back at what happened and want more than just okay. Don't you?"

Jack didn't answer because he knew that his dad was talking about more than his own life. Jack loved his job as much as his dad had, and he also realized he had the same tendencies to be absorbed in work rather than life beyond the clinic. What he hadn't figured out was what to do about that. How to find the right balance so that he lived his life instead of just going through the motions.

"So what's this about? All these questions?" his dad asked, placing the piece of wood on the bench and covering it with a tarp.

"My job takes up all my time, just like yours did. And I love my job, just like you. But I lost my wife because of it, so I'm alone. No family. And I don't want to wake up one day and wonder if I missed out on something that might have been special if I had been paying more attention to my personal life."

His dad clapped him on his shoulder. "You want Aunt Sarah to fix you up? I'm sure she's got plenty of candidates for you."

Jack shuddered. "I don't know how to find the right balance between my job and my life, so anyone she introduced me to now would end up leaving me in the end anyway. They always do."

"Maybe this is something you should also talk to your mom about. She might have a different perspective than I do."

"Yeah, I guess."

"And don't tell her about the Christmas gift, okay?"

MELANIE SPENT HER Sunday afternoon updating her online dating profile again. She'd added the picture from Jack's phone, then searched through the probable matches, but none of the men appealed to her. She lowered the lid of her laptop and placed the computer next to her on the bed. She had set up a date with someone for that evening, but she debated whether to cancel or not. Blind dating didn't seem to be working for her, and online dating wasn't doing much better. Maybe she'd be better off doing something else that actually appealed to her. Like a long soak in her bathtub with a book.

She glanced at her phone, but no one had called or texted. Not Marius. Not even Jack. But then he usually spent his Sunday afternoons at his parents' house with his family. He'd even invited her a few times to accompany him. But being around his immediate family made her feel only more alone. It was one thing to be around the entire Cuthbert family with so much noise and activity going on that she enjoyed it. Spending time with just his parents and his sister with her family only showed her that she'd never have what she truly wanted: Jack.

She waved her hands in front of her.

Enough of that thinking. She needed to get past Jack. And hanging out last night with him had helped a little. They'd fallen back into their usual habits easily. She didn't want to lose that with him because then she'd have nothing at all with him. And that wasn't an option.

Her phone buzzed. She glanced at it. A text from her date canceling with a promise to reschedule. Relief flooded her, and she responded back with a quick Ok. Talk to you soon.

With an open evening ahead of her, she leaned back on the tufted headboard and considered her options. She could text Shelby and see if she wanted to catch a movie. She typed out a quick invitation, then lay back on her pillow. Since she'd gotten involved with Josh, Shelby hadn't been as available for getting together. Not that she blamed her friend since her relationship with her new husband was obviously important. Mel only hoped that she and Shelby would still find enough time to get together and enjoy each other's company the way they'd always done.

Her phone rang minutes after sending

the text invite. "Hey, Mel. I can't see a movie tonight. Josh and I are looking at houses today. We've seen one that's a possibility, but I like the look of this next one we're going to see."

"Oh, that's right. I completely forgot about that."

"While I have you on the phone, how did the date with Marius go last night?"

Mel paused as she reviewed the previous evening. "It didn't. He didn't show up, then texted to say he'd had a family emergency."

"Oh, Mel."

"It's okay. Jack showed up while I was waiting for him, and we had a good talk. We're going to be okay now." Silence on the other end. "Really, Shelby. It was a good talk, and we decided that our friendship is too important to risk losing it over anything else."

"You decided or Jack did?"

"We both did. We're okay. I'm okay."

"You don't sound too excited about that."

"He doesn't love me like that, so I'm accepting that and moving on. It's okay. Really."

"You keep saying *okay*, but I'm not convinced that you are."

Mel sighed and placed the phone between her ear and shoulder. "Maybe this was the push I needed to finally get over him and find someone who loves me back."

"Maybe." Shelby paused on the other end, and Mel could hear Josh saying something to her. "Listen, we just pulled up to the next house. I'll call you later, okay?"

Mel hung up and placed the phone on the bed next to her computer. The dog raised his head to look at her, then laid it back down. So plans with Shelby were out. Jack was at his parents. And the thought of lining up another date at the last minute didn't appeal. She groaned and got off the bed. She didn't need someone else to fill her time. She was an independent woman who could find something to amuse herself.

The cover of a book she'd brought home from her store filled her head. Yes. That was the ticket. She'd escape into someone else's life for a few hours and find contentment there.

JACK RINSED OFF a plate and placed it in the dishwasher rack as his mom wiped down the stove with a dishrag. "Thank you for helping me clean the kitchen, sweetie."

"Of course." He ran the water over a handful of utensils. "Actually, I was hoping that the two of us could talk while we work."

In his peripheral vision, he saw his mom's hand still. "What did you want to talk about?"

He turned off the faucet and left the sink to face her. "How did you make your marriage with Dad work?"

Her eyebrows shot up into her hairline. "I wasn't expecting that question. What brought this on? You thinking about Stacey?"

His ex-wife had been on his mind, but not for the reason his mother probably assumed. "I'm just wondering how you and Dad made everything work when he was gone all the time. Because let's not pretend that my job didn't break up my marriage."

"Is that what you think happened?"

"Mom, that is what happened. Stacey told me that I was married more to my job than I was to her, and she wanted out." He could remember the night he'd returned home from work to find his wife sitting on the sofa, her purse and a suitcase sitting next to her. He didn't think he'd ever forget that night. "So how did you make it work with Dad and his job?"

"Are you thinking of getting married again? I didn't even know you were dating someone."

Leave it up to his mom to jump to that conclusion. "No, I'm not dating. And you haven't answered my question."

"When two people want to make their marriage succeed, it's all about the give and take. And don't fool yourself into thinking that it always has to be fifty-fifty. Some of the time you give more. Others you take more." She leaned past Jack to rinse her dishcloth under the faucet before wringing it out and laying it flat to dry on the edge of the sink. She turned to look at him. "But it really comes down to priorities. If you want to make it work, you will. And your partner will do the same."

"Dad didn't seem to work on your marriage. He was rarely home."

"But when he was, he was completely present and very attentive. I held on to those moments for the times I was alone. And I knew it was only temporary."

"He was police chief for almost twenty years. How is that temporary?"

"And he's been retired the last two, and we're having the time of our lives now." She put a hand on his shoulder. "You kids these days think that you have to have everything right in the moment. But there's something to be said for appreciating what you wait for. And trust me, all those years he was gone are worth the time we have together now."

Jack considered her words, but shook his head. "So if I want to make a relationship work, I have to wait until I retire? That's too long for me to wait."

"All I'm saying is that if you had wanted things to work out with Stacey, you would have made the sacrifices necessary to do so. But how many times did she ask you to cut your hours at work? And how many times did you try it for a week or two but then went back to your usual on call twenty-four seven?"

"I was trying to get my practice off the ground, Mom. That wasn't the time for me to be cutting my hours."

"And you chose your job over your relationship with your wife. Her priority was spending time with you, but yours was building the business. If you really wanted to make things work with her, you would have changed your focus. That's why it didn't work out."

He sighed, knowing she was right. "So if I had convinced her to hold on a little longer, then we'd still be together?"

"No, she was going to leave you eventually."

He frowned at her words. "Thanks, Mom."

His mom peered at him, and he felt as if he was five years old again and she was asking if he'd been the one who had broken the vase in the living room. She'd always had a way of looking at him to get to the truth of a situation. "She wasn't the right woman for you, Jack. We both know that."

He hadn't known it then, and there were still times that he wasn't sure about that. Instead of disagreeing with her, he leaned against the counter and crossed his arms over his chest. "Sometimes I feel like I'm meant to be alone. That the satisfaction I find in my career is enough for me."

"But is it? I don't think you'd be asking these questions if you really believed that."

ANGELIQUE FINALLY TOOK his phone call the following evening, but drew the line at meeting in person. "No offense, Jack, but I don't see any point in getting together to discuss a relationship that's been a long time over and done, do you?"

He guessed that he didn't, but he wouldn't have minded seeing her. Angelique had been one of the As that he had imagined getting serious with one day, but that day never came for them. Instead, she had found someone else shortly after they broke up. Last he heard, they were still together.

"How are you and Wes doing?" he asked her.

"Wonderful. We're getting married next April."

"That's fantastic news. I'm happy that you found someone." And he truly was. She deserved to be happy, and if that was with Wes, then he could congratulate her on finding the right one to spend her life with. "Did you ever wonder what would have happened if we had worked out?"

"Not really. You might have been interested in me, but your heart really wasn't in the relationship."

That wasn't the way he remembered it. He remembered thinking that she was the kindest, most compassionate woman he'd ever met. That she had a beauty that radiated from the inside and made her glow. That she was exactly what he wanted in a future wife. "Why would you say that? I thought we had a pretty good time together."

"Having a good time doesn't mean that we were supposed to be together."

Didn't it? He mentally reviewed his relationships and discovered that he had enjoyed his time with the women and had thought that fact meant they should be in a relationship. "I don't know about that. I figured that you might be the one I could go the distance with."

Angelique sighed. "Oh, Jack. It takes more than enjoying time spent together to make a good relationship. I thought you would have found that out by now."

"Okay. So what does make a good relationship? You and Wes, for example. What makes the two of you work?"

"We're honest with each other, first of all. We respect each other and give space where needed." She paused as if thinking more about it. "We have the same values and want the same things for our lives. Every hour we spend with each other doesn't need to be exciting or even interesting. But it also takes time to build that relationship."

"And we didn't have that?"

"In order to be honest with me, you had to be honest with yourself first."

"I always told you the truth."

"If that's so, then let me ask you this. How is your friendship with Melanie going?"

Mel again? Why did her name keep coming up with everyone? "We're good."

"Still just friends?"

"My relationship with Mel had nothing to do with our time together." Did it? "She wasn't a factor in how I felt about you."

"You need to face the fact that Melanie has never been or will never be just a friend. If anyone has been your soul mate, it's her. And until you can confront that truth, then any relationship you pursue with another woman is doomed."

After he hung up the phone with Angelique, he sat on his sofa and considered her words. She was wrong. Melanie was only his friend. Despite what Mel wanted, he didn't have those kinds of feelings for her. That was the truth, as much as it might hurt her.

Did he love her? Of course he did. But like a friend.

His phone barked with a notification. He peeked at the screen, then started shaking his head. The dating app had sent him a notification that he'd been matched at a 92 percent probability with another app user named Melanie Beach. There couldn't be two of them, could there?

CHAPTER SIX

JACK SIPPED HIS usual coffee and leaned on the counter at the bookstore as Mel worked the coffee bar. It had been over a week since she had reconciled with him, and things were good between them. Almost back to the normal they'd had before. It had also been over a week since the dating app had matched the two of them up, but he hadn't brought that up with her and she hadn't mentioned it either. Maybe she thought like he did that it was best that they forget that.

"Do you have a date tonight after you close the store?" Jack asked her.

Melanie paused as she prepared the next coffee drink for a customer. After handing the latte to the customer, she stood in front of him and wiped the counter down with a bar mop. "Not tonight. You thinking about grabbing some dinner?"

"Only if you consider a huge tub of pop-corn with gargantuan amounts of cola an appropriate dinner. That new superhero movie finally came out this past week-end, and we've been talking about going for months. Let's go see it. There's a seven-thirty showing we could make."

Mel considered her evening plans and admitted that going to see a movie was far more enjoyable than going through her closet to find items she no longer wanted to wear and would donate to the local women's shelter. "I'll have to pick up the dog and take him home first, but that sounds like a great idea. You buy the tickets, and I'll buy the snacks."

Jack grinned. "It's a date." His smile fal-tered. "I meant, okay, we'll go. Not that this is a date. We're going to be sitting to-gether, but it's not an actual date." He ran a hand over his face. "I stepped into that one, didn't I?"

She chuckled and shook her head. Maybe he hadn't forgotten they'd been matched. "You really did mess that one up. But it's okay. I knew what you meant."

He seemed to wilt with relief. "Good.

I'll check out the new books section while you finish up here."

Later, they took their popcorn and drinks into the theater and found their seats halfway up the auditorium in the center of the aisle. Since it was a Tuesday night, there were plenty of empty seats. Mel tossed a few kernels into her mouth. "My dad called last night." Her father had retired three years ago and moved to Florida with her new stepmother. "They won't be coming back to Michigan for Thanksgiving." Which had led to them disagreeing again over the phone. "I told him that he never makes an effort to see me at the holidays. And he knows that I can't get away then, since it's my busiest time of the year."

"And what did he say to that?"

"That marriage is hard enough without trying to appease his grown daughter who is old enough not to need him. So I told him that I've always needed him, but he was too wrapped up in his relationships to notice. I offered to visit them after the holidays, but he wasn't interested." She sighed as Jack snuck her a look, and she waved off the concern. "It's fine. It's not like he usually spends the holidays with me anyway." She couldn't even remember the last holiday they'd spent together as a family.

"You know you're always welcome at Christopher and Penny's house for the day. In fact, Penny asked me to ask you. And rumor has it that we're going to try deep frying a turkey this year."

She looked over at him. "Shelby said the same thing, but I don't know. Maybe I shouldn't."

"What's not to know? Where else would you go?"

She had thought about spending the day getting the store ready for the huge Black Friday sale. She could pick up a rotisserie chicken Wednesday night and save it for the next day. She wasn't a big fan of turkey as it was, so that sounded like a better plan. She'd have the store to herself and could spend the afternoon decorating it for the holidays. She couldn't always depend on the Cuthbert family as her backup holiday plans. Maybe it was time she put some distance between them.

Jack tossed a popcorn kernel at her. "Earth to Mel. What are you thinking?"

"Maybe I should pass."

"And miss Aunt June's famous cranberry cake? Are you kidding me?"

"It's nice that your family includes me, but—"

"Nice? They love you as if you were one of us."

"But I'm not one of you." The words came out soft because she didn't want them to shatter even as her heart ached inside her chest.

Jack put his arm around her shoulder and pulled her closer to his side. "Don't let your dad ruin your Thanksgiving. If nothing else, I want you there. It wouldn't be my favorite holiday without you."

She looked into his eyes and saw the sincerity of his words. She gave a soft nod. "I'll think about it."

Jack smiled, and she rested her head on his shoulder as the lights dimmed and the previews began. By the end of the movie, the superhero defeated the villain, and a surprise twist set up the next movie. As the lights rose, they gathered what remained of their snacks and walked down the stairs and out of the auditorium. Outside, the temperature had dropped while they'd been in the movie, and Mel gathered the edges of her jacket closer around her. "Thanks for suggesting the movie tonight. It was just what I needed."

"I can't believe we have to wait at least a year to find out what happens next though." He hit the button on his key fob, and his car's lights blinked.

They walked down the aisle to where their cars were parked side by side. Mel unlocked her car door and leaned against the frame, watching Jack. If this had been a real date, would he try to kiss her? Would he come home with her? She shook her head at the thoughts. This wasn't a date. This was just two friends enjoying their favorite action movie franchise. "We'll have to go see it when the next one comes out."

"It's a date." He groaned. "You know what I mean."

She leaned in and gave his cheek a peck. "I do. Good night." She opened her car door, but didn't get inside. Instead, she turned to face Jack. "You know, I think I will come to Penny's on Thanksgiving."

Jack smiled at her. "I was hoping you'd say that."

"But you have to come help me decorate the store after dinner."

He let out a chuckle. "It's a deal." He gave her a quick hug though she tried to hang on to him just a moment longer. "Text me when you get home so I know you arrived safe."

It was their typical farewell, and she nodded. "You too."

Once she reached home, she texted Jack. Then sat on her bed and wondered how long it would take to be truly over him.

JACK WEAVED THROUGH the crowded bar and found Amanda sitting on the far side, her chin resting on her hand as her long blond hair fell forward over one shoulder. He took a seat across from her. "Thank you for meeting me."

"I'll admit that I was intrigued by your cryptic voicemail. I didn't think we had any unfinished business to go over."

He looked across at her and wondered why things hadn't worked out with her. Their relationship had started off wonderful. So much so that he wondered if he might get married again. But as they always did, Amanda broke up with him, and he was left single. Again. "I'm trying to get some perspective on my relationships. And you know how they say hindsight is twenty-twenty."

"Perspective? Or closure?"

"Maybe a little bit of both?"

Amanda took a deep breath and folded her hands on the tabletop. "You said you had some questions for me."

Obviously, she wasn't wondering why they'd ever broken up. Or at least she seemed resolute in her decision to. He was about to ask her when the server placed their drinks in front of them. The server looked between them. "Are we ordering food tonight, folks?"

Amanda shook her head. "I won't be here that long." She waved a hand at him. "But go ahead, if you're hungry."

He was, but he didn't want to eat alone in a bar. He'd find something later on the way home. "I'm fine. Thanks."

After the server left, Jack watched as Amanda took a sip of her drink, her eyes on his. He waited until she placed the glass on the table to ask, "Why didn't things work out with us?"

She frowned as if surprised by the question. "That's what you want to know? You know why we didn't work out. Your job consumed your every minute. And I don't play second fiddle to that."

"Good. I mean, that's what I figured." He let out a sigh. He slid his beer closer to him. "Thank you for your honesty."

"Of course." She gazed at him. "So are you seeing anyone right now?"

He shook his head, then looked across the room to find Melanie sitting with a man. She laughed at something he said and pushed her hair behind her ear. He frowned and stared at them as the guy reached across the table to put his hand on hers. Was she out on another internet date? He turned to look at the guy who made his lip curl and gave him a shudder. He didn't know the guy, but he had a bad feeling about him.

Amanda cleared her throat, and he faced her. "Sorry. I got sidetracked for a moment."

She glanced to where his gaze had been, then turned back, her cheeks turning red. "Oh, you've got to be joking." She stood and started to gather her purse and coat. "I should have known. It's always about Melanie."

Jack jumped up, embarrassed and confused. "Amanda, please. I do want to talk more about this."

"There's no point." She stuffed her arms into the coat and zipped it up. "Why don't you finally admit that you're in love with her? She always came first in our relationship. Even over your job, if you want to really get to the heart of the problem." She put her purse over her shoulder. "Don't call me again. In fact, erase my number." She grabbed her drink and downed the last of it.

"It's not what you think. I didn't know she'd be here tonight."

Amanda rolled her eyes, then left Jack standing there, disbelieving how the conversation had gone so wrong. He'd been looking in Melanie's direction, but that's all he'd been doing. He sat down again and took a sip of his beer before letting his gaze drift to the table across the room. The guy was leaning forward now, feeding Mel something. She chewed. Frowned. Then started to cough and took a gulp from her drink.

Jack watched as she continued coughing. No, not coughing. Choking. Without thinking, he stood and dashed across the room. Stood behind Mel and placed his hands under her rib cage. Pushed up until she coughed up something that fell onto the table. Kept his arms around her in case she was still choking and he'd need to apply more pressure. "Are you okay, Mel?"

She wheezed for a moment, then shifted to look at him. "Okay, I think. Thank you, Jack."

He nodded and dropped his hands from her. "I didn't mean to interrupt your date."

Mel waved off his apology.

The guy peered at him suspiciously. "Wait. Do you two know each other?"

She motioned with her thumb toward him. "This is my best friend Jack who I was telling you about earlier."

The guy straightened and held out his hand. "And I'm Cole. Her date tonight."

Jack shook the hand, then looked at the table and noticed the food on their plates. "You're allergic to shellfish, so why would you eat some from his fork?" He pointed to the food like a detective who'd just discovered whodunit.

Melanie put a hand to her lips and glanced at her date. "Shellfish?"

The guy grimaced. "The mushrooms must be stuffed with crab. I didn't know you were allergic."

Of course he didn't. But Jack did. He turned his gaze back to her. "Maybe we should have you checked out at the hospital."

Mel took a step away from him and closer to the table. "I'm fine now. I don't think it's necessary, do you?"

"It wouldn't hurt, would it?"

The guy took a closer step to Mel. "Jack is right. Maybe you should get checked out. Just in case."

Jack motioned over his shoulder. "My car is right outside. I can take you."

"Actually if anyone is going to take her, it will be me since she's my date for the night." Cole put a hand on her elbow. "Shall we go, Melanie?"

"Hey, you fed her shellfish which made her choke. And you've had—" he peered at the table again, counting the empty glasses in front of the guy's chair "—three drinks. I've only had a sip, so I will drive her since I'm her sober best friend. Understood, Cole?"

"I understand that you're trying to horn in on my evening with my date, Jack. She's here at my invitation, so I will drive her."

Melanie shrugged out of Cole's grip and glared at Jack. "I'm not going anywhere with either one of you because I'm perfectly fine. Which you two might have noticed if you weren't acting like children and arguing." She slipped on her coat and pulled her phone from her purse. "So good evening to you both. I'll order an Uber to take me home."

Jack watched her leave the bar. When he turned to Cole, the other man glowered at him. "She was the first date that wasn't a disaster in the last three weeks, and you ruined it, pal." He crumpled into his chair and emptied his drink.

Jack swallowed and realized that he'd ruined the date for Melanie too. He returned to his table, placed a few bills on it for his and Amanda's drinks as well as a handsome tip for the server, then left the bar. He found her standing just outside the front door, next to a grinning turkey sitting on a hay bale, her arms crossed. She glanced at him, then shook her head. "I'm not going to the emergency room, so you can get that idea out of your head."

Jack held up his hand. "You should go back to your date. I won't bother you anymore tonight."

He started to walk toward his car, but heard Melanie call his name. He turned to find her following him. "Could I get a ride home?"

"No. Go back inside."

"Why?"

"You looked like you were having a good time. Before the choking, I mean."

She peered at him. "Why were you here tonight?"

"I met with Amanda. It did not go well."

"Still trying to figure out what went wrong with your relationships?" Her know-

SYNDI POWELL 189

ing expression was easy to spot. "Why are you doing this?"

"Something Shelby said to me made me wonder why my past relationships haven't worked out, but it doesn't matter." He looked behind her at the bar. "Go back inside. Please. I feel bad enough that I ruined your date."

She put a hand on his arm. "You didn't ruin it. It wasn't going that great anyway. Cole is a little too in love with himself."

"He seemed to think that it was going well."

She gave a shrug. "Like you said, it doesn't matter." She looked toward his car. "I don't want to wait out in the cold, and the Uber app said it's going to be at least another fifteen minutes before a car can get here. Do you mind giving me a ride home?"

MEL KEPT HER gaze out the windshield as Jack drove them to her house. She couldn't look at him. Couldn't tell him how relieved she'd been that he'd arrived when he had. And not just because she'd been choking. Cole had been stuffy and a little pompous, suggesting that she try some of his stuffed mushrooms when she hadn't been interested. To see Jack coming to her literal and figurative rescue had felt almost like a fairy-tale ending to their story. But then he'd gotten all overprotective, trying to put himself between her and her date when it hadn't been his place. And any romantic feelings she might have had turned to frustration because she could take care of herself, thank you very much.

She curled her hands into fists and gave a soft moan.

Jack glanced at her. "I knew I should have driven you to the emergency room."

He hit his turn signal as if meaning to turn them around, but she put a hand on his arm. "I'm fine, Jack. Just a little overwrought after this evening. It didn't exactly go the way I expected."

He peered at her, then gave a short nod. "If you change your mind, call me and I'll drive you."

"I won't change my mind."

They fell silent once more until her stomach made a loud grumbling noise.

Jack glanced at her, then shook his head. "Hungry?"

"Starving actually. I barely ate any of my dinner."

He pulled into the drive-through line at a nearby fast-food restaurant. "How about if we make it something quick to eat?"

When he reached the lit-up menu with the speaker, he gave an order and doubled it but stopped when she put a hand on his arm. "I'll take a grilled chicken sandwich instead. No fries. And a side salad with ranch dressing."

He turned back and changed her order before pulling forward to the cashier. When he got to the window, he paid for their meals and handed her the bags full of food to hold in her lap. She pulled out a few French fries and fed them to him as he drove back to her place, eating a couple of them herself to stave off her hunger. "Hey, you said no fries."

She blinked her eyes at him several times. "You would deny me a few fries after choking earlier tonight?"

He grinned at her words, and she handed him a few more fries.

Once they got to her place, they didn't make it as far as the kitchen table but plopped down on the sofa in the living room and ate with their fingers. She unwrapped her sandwich and took a bite, then glanced at the juices dripping down Jack's arm. Man, that hamburger looked good. But she had wanted to do something different. The dog sat, and was watching them eat, hoping for a crumb or two to fall.

Once they'd eaten, she gathered the wrappers and stuffed them in the bag. Jack lay back against the sofa and put one hand on his belly, the other petting the dog. "That was good." He looked up at her. "How was your chicken sandwich?"

"Really good, actually. I'm glad I decided to try something different."

He looked her over. "You're doing a lot of that lately."

"I didn't like my life the way it was, so I had to do something about it."

"And how is that working out for you?"

She gave a shrug and leaned back into the sofa pillows. "Not sure yet. Some things are good, but others I'd rather not repeat. Like the guy I met tonight."

"You're still online dating?"

"And you're still consulting with the As about went wrong with your relationships?"

He gave a soft nod. "Next up is Stacey. That is, if she'll answer my calls."

Mel tried to keep her face neutral. She hadn't been a fan of Stacey's ever since Jack had introduced them when he moved back to Thora after graduating college. Her first impression of the woman made her think that Stacey was only in the relationship for what she could get out of it. Then Melanie had liked her even less after the divorce. She hated to see how much pain Jack had been in at the time. "Offer to buy her dinner at an expensive restaurant that has tablecloths and a fancy wine list."

"Already did, but still no response." He looked her over once again. "Are you feeling okay? No aftereffects of the seafood?"

She rolled her head in his direction to look at him. "Nothing. I'm perfectly fine."

He put an arm around her and pulled her close so that her head rested on his shoulder. "You gave me quite a scare, Mel. I don't know what I'd do if something happened to you, and I lost you for good."

She gave him a nudge in the ribs. "I feel the same way about you." She rose on her elbow and looked into his eyes, hoping to see that his feelings for her had changed. But he was still Jack. Still looking at her as if they were only friends. No burning lust in those baby blues. She sighed and lay back down. "Thank you for saving me."

"From the seafood or from the date?"

She started to giggle, then let it grow into a belly laugh. Jack joined in.

THE GROCERY STORE intercom was playing Christmas carols as Jack wandered through the crowded aisles. Before going home for the night, he wanted to pick up a few items to bring to the Cuthbert family Thanksgiving the next day. Other shoppers had their carts full of food they'd be sharing with their families and friends while he could hold the stuff that he needed in his arms.

He'd already chosen a couple of pies but turned down the snack aisle, figuring some salty chips would be good for that evening's dinner. A woman with long blond hair bumped into him as he rounded the corner. "Oof." He reached out with his free arm to steady her. "Are you all right?" The woman turned her face to him, and he felt his jaw drop. "Stacey."

His ex-wife appeared even better than the last time he'd seen her in the courtroom as the judge signed their divorce decree. She'd never looked at him while the judge ended that part of his life. Now, she stared up at him and smiled. "Hey, Jack." She looked behind him. "Where's Mel?"

He frowned. "Why would she be here with me?"

"I heard that you two were together." She paused and focused on his face. "You have told her how you felt, haven't you? She's the reason we're not together after all."

Not this again. "As I recall, you said it was my career and how I was never at home."

"No, what I said was that you always had something more important than me. Your job. Melanie. Your family." She cocked her head to one side. "Don't tell me that you let her slip through your fingers."

"Fine. Then I won't say a word."

"Oh, Jack." She put a hand on his arm and rubbed it up to his shoulder before letting her hand linger there. "I thought you would have gotten wise before now."

"I'm trying to learn from my mistakes in the past. It's why I've been trying to reach you, but you haven't answered the voice-mails I left."

"Why did you call me?"

Stacey gave him the once-over, and he wondered how he compared to when they'd been married. He worked out more often, so he knew he was fitter. And the short beard was new too. He gave her the once-over too. She looked better than good. She wore her hair longer. Had on more makeup while he preferred the more natural look like Mel usually wore. But Stacey made it all come together. "You seem...happy," he said.

She smiled. "I am finally. It took me a long time to get over you. But I'm in a good place now. Content, you know? You?"

He shrugged, then moved closer to her when another shopper tried to squeeze past them. The scent Stacey wore smelled lovely too. "I'm good. Got a partner in the clinic so I'm not there all the time."

"You needed that years ago. You work too hard."

"That part hasn't changed, but I'm trying to find more balance in my life."

She smiled again, and he felt the kick in the stomach he'd always felt when she'd done that before. A flicker of attraction flared in his chest. He looked around. "I don't see Neil with you."

She gave a shrug. "We broke up a couple months ago. The divorce will be final in the New Year."

"I'm sorry to hear that."

Another shopper tried to move past them, and Jack put an arm around Stacey's waist and moved her closer so there was room in the aisle. "Sorry," he mumbled again, trying to ignore the red flags that were waving as she giggled. "This place is a little crazy right now. Want to go get a drink? Catch up? Maybe have that talk like I've been calling about?"

She nodded. "I'd like that."

And so they met up at the pub around

the corner from the grocery store. He ordered her a white wine spritzer along with his beer. She smiled. "You remembered my drink."

"I think you'd be surprised by how much I remember about you." And he did remember a lot. He remembered how she had always run into his arms to greet him, kissing him until he'd been breathless. There had been fireworks every time they embraced. A white-hot passion that seemed to consume them, even toward the end before she left. Maybe that's why her leaving had come as such a shock.

She reached over and put her hand on his. "I've missed you, Jack."

He held her hand gently. "I've missed you too. Now tell me what you've been up to."

For the next hour, she regaled him with stories about her fledgling interior design business and some of the more colorful clients. He told her stories about the animals he cared for and their misadventures. They discussed news events and popular culture, but they avoided anything that touched on Neil or Mel.

Stacey checked her watch and winced.

"I didn't realize it was this late. I need to get going." She stood, and he rose to his feet, helping her with her coat. When she turned to face him, he found himself staring into her eyes. She put a hand on his chest. "Listen, I know we didn't work out before, but I've learned that I need to be more flexible in my relationships. To give allowances for my partner. This is going to sound strange, and maybe it's because of the holidays and we're both alone, but I'm wondering if we could try dating again."

He swallowed and fought for an answer. Try again? More red flags waved accompanied by the annoying shrill of a siren.

But she was right. It was the holidays. It might be nice to have someone to spend them with. He squeezed her fingers in his and ignored the image of Mel. She was moving on. He should see if Stacey was right. Maybe they could make it work this time.

He cleared his throat, which seemed to be clogged. "I'd like that."

THE LIGHTS WENT up in the movie theater, and Mel sighed in relief. She stood and retrieved her coat as her date that evening did the same. What had she thought would happen when she'd agreed to see the same movie she'd seen with Jack only days earlier? She'd thought that Brendan seemed nice, and he had been eager to see the superhero film. She had enjoyed the movie the first time around and figured she'd like seeing it again.

If only her date had restrained himself from narrating the entire story to her. Or eating all the popcorn.

"That was something, wasn't it?" Brendan asked as they placed their empty drinks and popcorn bucket into the trash can at the front of the theater before exiting. "I can't wait until the next one comes out."

"Me either."

"We should plan on seeing it together then."

Mel turned to peer at him. "Do you always plan things so far in advance?"

"Sure do. I'm a planner by nature. Even planned my own kindergarten graduation. Got off to an early start. What about you, Melissa?"

She turned back to look at him, stepping out of the way of another couple who walked past. "Um, I do like to be organized, especially with my shop, but I'm not a huge planner."

He gave a shrug. "And yet, we seemed to click through email. Pretty cool, huh?"

This guy was nice, but talk about no chemistry. Unfortunately, she had no interest in pursuing anything with him. "So, are you thinking what I'm thinking?"

Mel racked her brain. What had they been talking about besides the movie? "About?"

"I know that June is traditional for weddings, but I've always been partial to the spring. Say late April or early May? What do you think, Melissa?"

Was he really starting to plan their wedding? "I think we should discuss a second date before there's any discussion regarding wedding plans."

He gave a shrug. "Of course, but I want to get a jump start. Places book up pretty fast around here. You can never start too early, is what I say."

"Listen here, Brandon—"

"It's Brendan."

"And I'm Melanie, not Melissa." She took a few more steps back from him and smiled. "You seem like a good guy and all, but this isn't really working for me. I'd rather us plan on not going on another date. Sorry."

He shrugged and smiled back. "I get it. I've got a whole week of other dates planned. Good luck, Melissa."

She was about to correct him again, but she just shook her head and walked on. The crisp night air would hopefully help her to clear her head.

It wasn't until she got home that she could find the humor in the situation. He'd wanted to start planning the wedding on the first date? She sent Jack a quick text to let him know she'd made it home okay.

Any sparks?

Mel winced at the thought of that. None. Although he tried to plan the next forty years of my life.

What?

She squelched her smile at Jack's confusion. I'm fine. It's fine. I'll fill you in another time.

Three dots appeared as if he was typing

her a response, but several minutes passed without a return text. She placed her phone on the counter as she started to pull ingredients out of the refrigerator. She'd promised Penny that she'd bring her famous pumpkin muffins with streusel topping to Thanksgiving dinner, a recipe that she'd inherited from her mother. And the muffins tasted better when prepared the night before.

She was elbow deep in mixing pumpkin puree with eggs when her phone dinged. She glanced at it and noticed that Jack had finally texted back. Wiping her hands on a dish towel before she picked up the phone, she wondered what had taken him so long.

I saw Stacey tonight.

Oh. She waited before typing a response, erasing and rewriting it several times to keep her reply casual and breezy though she felt anything but. How is she?

Good. Still beautiful. Getting divorced again.

Mel wasn't surprised by that development. She suspected that Stacey had been seeing someone else before she officially broke things off with Jack. Not that Mel had any proof. Just a gut feeling. Sorry to hear that.

She might not be best buddies with Stacey, but no one deserved to go through the pain of a second divorce.

She wants to get back together.

The breath caught in Mel's throat. What? Why would you even consider that?

So much for casual and breezy. Didn't he remember how it was after Stacey had left him? How he had spent weeks and months on her couch crying on her shoulder? How he had vowed that he could never marry again? Mel had been the one to help him pick up the pieces of his shattered heart. Who had been beside him every step of rebuilding his self-confidence. Who had cheered when he'd started dating again and told her he could possibly see a relationship in his future.

Okay, maybe *cheered* was too strong of a word. Regretted that he hadn't seen her as a potential date instead. Longed for him to notice her finally as a romantic partner. And nursed her hurting heart when he'd dated the As.

She waited for Jack's response, but no text came.

What was he thinking about getting back together with Stacey? She knew that he was lonely, but she would never have expected him to go back to his ex-wife. She picked up her spatula to mix the batter with a renewed vigor.

Her phone rang, but she didn't need to look at the readout to know it was Jack. Wiping her hands off again, she took a deep breath before answering. "Why in the world would you let her back into your life?"

"I loved her."

"Loved. Past tense, Jack." She put the phone on speaker and began chopping. "What if she hurts you again?"

"What if it works out this time?"

Silence descended on them for a moment until Jack admitted, "I felt that familiar spark between us."

"You two always had chemistry, but is that enough? Changes or not, what happens when she's grown tired of you and your choice of spending long hours at the clinic? Don't think it hasn't gone unnoticed that you're there a lot, even with the new assistant vet."

A pause until he let out a puff of air. "I know you're right."

"I sense a *but* coming."

"But you don't know what it's like when the two of us are together." He halted for a moment. "It was just like old times."

"Well, aren't you only thinking of the good times right now? You need to remember the reality. You need to remember the bad ones too."

"I couldn't forget those even if I tried." He sighed on the other end. "You're right. I'm not thinking clearly about her just now. I should chalk this up to finding closure with Stacey once and for all."

"It might be for the best." She couldn't stand to see him get hurt a second time by Stacey. No matter what he might think, the woman wasn't good for him. Or his heart. "You need to find the right woman. And I know she's out there somewhere." She truly believed that, even if it wasn't her.

"It's hard to be alone during the holidays, you know?"

Mel certainly did. She'd spent enough of them on her own. But she didn't remind Jack of that fact. Instead she made a noise of agreement.

He cleared his throat. "You're still coming to Penny and Christopher's tomorrow?"

"I wouldn't miss it for the world. There's nothing like a Cuthbert family holiday."

CHAPTER SEVEN

SNOWFLAKES DRIFTED DOWN from the metal-gray sky as Jack watched his father drop the thawed turkey into the boiling peanut oil. Pops and hisses emitted from the deep pot, sending off a few sparks and flickers of the open flame underneath. Jack and his uncles took a few steps back just in case the bird burst into flames. Uncle Mark, the former fire chief of Thora and a current fire inspector for the state of Michigan, waved them back over. "It's not going to catch fire. We'll be fine."

Jack joined his cousin Penny's husband at the patio table. "Thirsty?" Christopher asked as he handed him a bottle of water.

Jack thanked him, then opened the bottle, taking a few sips. He turned and looked behind him through the glass door to see Melanie chatting with his mom. She laughed at something she said, throwing her head back. He smiled in response and turned to find Christopher watching him. "Penny said that there was something between you and Melanie, but I wasn't sure about that until now."

Jack almost choked on his water. He coughed and took a few deep breaths. "What are you talking about?"

Christopher motioned with his head toward the patio door. "You and Mel. I insisted that the two of you were just friends, but my wife seemed convinced that there was something more there between you both."

"You were right the first time. We're just friends."

Christopher smirked at him. "Like Penny and I were just friends only a year ago?" He shook his head. "I saw that look on your face just now. And it was definitely more than friendship."

Jack winced. He didn't know what Christopher seemed to think he saw, but he had been watching Mel with his mom. Period. End of story. He heard Mel laugh again, and his gaze was drawn to the glass door.

"Yep. You've got it bad."

He forced his attention back to his cousin's husband. "You don't understand. I can't have those kinds of feelings for her."

"I do understand. In fact, I said those same words about Penny. But then I married her." Christopher patted him on the shoulder as he rose to his feet. "Don't worry. Your secret is safe with me."

"But there is no secret." There couldn't be one because Jack didn't feel that way. He put his head in his hands. He didn't, right?

He felt a hand on his shoulder and turned to find Mel smiling down at him. Man, she was gorgeous without even trying. Her new haircut framed those big brown eyes that a man could get lost in. Or at least, a different man than Jack could, he reminded himself. "Having fun?" he asked her.

She took the seat next to his, smiling. "Your mom was just telling me about when you used to insist that turkeys said wobble, wobble because of all the food you eat at Thanksgiving." She nudged his side. "She also told me about the year that you and Penny hid in the attic."

He nodded. His aunt had died when

Penny was just a baby, so she felt the loss of her mother acutely during the holidays. He had noticed that his youngest cousin was missing just before dinner and had found her in the attic looking through a box of her mother's things. He sat next to her and held her hand when she sobbed. "I do remember that."

She leaned her head on his shoulder. "You've always had such a good heart. First with your family. Now also with your animals."

He swallowed as the scent of her met his nostrils. She smelled like lavender and vanilla, a potent combination that had him moving closer to her. "I think my dad hoped that I'd be more of a rough-and-tumble boy and have less of a soft heart. Maybe that's why I joined every sports team I could."

"Well, I wouldn't change a thing about you." She turned her head to grin at him. "What was it that you said to me before?" She glanced off in the distance, then brought her eyes back to him. "Ah, yes. To me, you're perfect."

His mouth had gone dry, and he reached over to grab his water bottle, quickly finishing it. "Any word on when dinner is going to be ready? I'm starving."

"Your sister brought a veggie tray. I can grab you some carrots and dip, if you want." She got to her feet. "Maybe another bottle of water too?"

"You don't have to do that. I can get it on my own."

"It would be my pleasure. Besides, I was thinking of getting some for myself. Be right back."

Jack thanked her, then turned to find Christopher looking at him, nodding and smiling.

BEFORE DINNER WAS SERVED, Mel found herself standing between Jack and Shelby's sister Laurel who had recently completed a stint in rehab and looked amazing. More than a decade earlier, Laurel had been in a car accident that had crushed her pelvis. After a year of surgeries, she'd found herself hooked on alcohol and pain medication. She'd gone to rehab then to get clean, but she had recently backslid into addiction. A mishap with her daughter had been the key to Laurel reaching out to get help from her family. "You're looking great," Mel told her.

Laurel smiled and wrapped her arms around her daughter Harper's shoulders to bring her closer. "Thank you. My sobriety is something to be truly thankful for this year. That and Harpie being well." She looked down at her daughter. "What are you thankful for, sweetie?"

"That we get to eat soon," the four-year-old whispered. "How much longer are the adults going to talk before we can finally eat?"

Penny's seven-year-old stepdaughter Daisy nodded in agreement.

Penny gave Daisy a wink before she tapped a knife on a crystal glass. "Before we start moving through the buffet line, I thought we'd follow the usual Cuthbert family tradition of sharing one thing we're thankful for this past year."

Harper huffed and folded her arms over her chest. Mel squelched a smile and listened as the Cuthbert family shared their blessings. There were the obvious ones about health and family and jobs with Great-aunt Sarah sharing that she was thankful that they hadn't lost power this year like they had the last Thanksgiving. When it was Shelby's turn, she put her arms around Josh's waist. "I'm thankful that Josh and his dad were willing to join us for Thanksgiving this year."

Josh smiled at her. "And I'm thankful that Shelby agreed to marry me."

A cry went up from Shelby's mother as she rushed forward to look at the ring on Shelby's finger. "But you're wearing a wedding band with the engagement ring already." She looked up at her daughter. "You're supposed to wait to wear that until after the wedding."

Shelby glanced at Josh who beamed at her. She turned back to look at her mother. "That's because I forgot to take it off this morning before we left the condo. I wasn't going to say anything until later, but since it's already out there… We got married when we were in Greece." She looked at the rest of the family and held out her arms. "Surprise!"

At the announcement, there was a moment of shock among the family before Shelby's dad stepped forward and shook Josh's hand. "Welcome to the family, son."

"Thank you, sir."

Then her dad turned and kissed Shelby on the cheek before hugging her tightly while the rest of her relatives surrounded them, trying to get closer to congratulate the couple. Jack leaned in toward Mel. "I'm glad she finally said something. I was starting to worry that I'd accidentally let it slip."

"From the way Shelby's dad reacted with such calm, I think Josh had already talked to him." He hadn't seemed to be that surprised by the announcement.

"I'm glad he followed my advice to talk to her dad and make sure he had his blessing before they announced it."

Mel felt her head jerk back as she turned to stare at him. "So now you're giving relationship advice? You?" Mel gave a laugh that seemed to start at her toes and bubble out the top.

He frowned at her laughter. "What's so funny about that?"

"You keep saying that you suck at relationships, but you gave Josh some really good advice about his own relationships with Shelby and your family." She eyed him, wondering what was happening with him. "I thought you had decided to stay out of it."

He shrugged, then leaned closer to her. His mouth was less than an inch from her ear, and she could feel his breath on her cheek. "I guess that your admission on Halloween changed something inside me. I guess I'm willing to consider a relationship again, and I'm thankful that we're back to being best friends."

Melanie nodded, but she really wanted to ask him why. Why couldn't he see that they deserved a shot to be together? Would he always see her as a friend and nothing more? She pasted a smile on her face and stepped away from the family circle. If anyone asked, she'd tell them she needed some fresh air as she walked through the kitchen and out the glass door to the patio.

Standing at the edge of the brick pavers where they met the lawn, she closed her eyes and took big gulps of the frigid air. She heard the patio door slide open and didn't need to turn to find out who had followed her. When Jack stood next to her, she blew out her breath. "I just need a moment."

"I know, dear."

She opened her eyes and turned to find not Jack, but Aunt Sarah by her side. "What are you doing out here without your coat? It's freezing."

Aunt Sarah motioned to her with a pointed look on her face. "I could ask you the same thing."

"You should go back inside. I'm fine. Really." But she wrapped her arms around her body to keep in what warmth she had.

"His eyes are opening, you know."

Mel frowned at the words, but she didn't need Aunt Sarah to explain what she meant. "But he still doesn't see anything beyond friendship with me. I don't think he ever will, and I'm a fool to keep hoping that will change."

"Are you absolutely sure about that?"

"I'm positive. He just thanked me for my friendship in there. It's never going to happen. And you know what I'm learning? I'm okay with that. I truly am. And I'm moving past him." She rubbed her arms. "You know, it really is cold out here. Maybe we should go back inside."

"I will when you do."

"Then let's go back in. I'm sure the family has congratulated Shelby and Josh by now." Mel looked at the older woman. "You figured their news out before the announcement, didn't you? You knew they were married already."

"And how would I know something like that?"

"Because you're very perceptive." Mel put her arm around Aunt Sarah's shoulders. "And Shelby has never been able to keep secrets from you."

Aunt Sarah laughed. "I guessed a few days ago, and she confirmed it. I think Josh will be good for this family. Shake it up a little. We were getting too set in our ways. Christopher complements us, but Josh will challenge." She started to walk back toward the house. "And I think you will become officially what we've always considered you. One of us."

"Thank you for your vote of confidence, but Jack has made up his mind about me. And it doesn't include romance."

"We'll see who's right, and my guess is that it won't take much longer."

JACK PUSHED BACK from the table and put his hands on his very full belly. "Man, I think the cooks outdid themselves this year. I don't think I could eat another bite."

"We haven't even brought out the desserts yet." Shelby wiped her mouth with her napkin and placed it crumpled on the table.

"Well, I didn't say that I didn't have room still for pumpkin pie. And I also brought pecan."

Mel shook her head at him, but he noticed the smile playing around her lips. She looked really good when she smiled at him like that. He leaned forward to tell her so when his phone started barking. His mom looked down the table at him, frowning. He pulled the phone from his pocket to put it on vibrate when he noticed the phone number. He answered it and stepped away from the table, walking down the hall toward the kitchen. "Lucas, what's wrong?"

"I know you're at your family dinner,

but Mrs. Danner called the emergency number. Her collie is in labor."

Jack winced as he walked into the kitchen. He'd known when he'd seen the dog earlier that week that she'd be having her puppies any day. "Well, you're the one on call today. I believe in you, you're a good vet. You can do it. Are you going over to see Winnie now?"

"But I've never done a caesarean section before. And figured it would be safer for me to do that at the office than on a house call."

"C-section?" He realized his voice had risen when the conversations in the other room paused. "Why would Winnie need a C-section?"

"Because Mrs. Danner said she's been in labor for hours but no puppies have been born. I'm concerned that there may be an issue."

Jack closed his eyes and rubbed his forehead. The longer the dog was in labor, the bigger an issue that could come later. He didn't have a choice. He had to leave his family, even if it was Thanksgiving. "Tell Mrs. Danner that I'm on my way to the clinic. I'll meet you all there, and you can assist. It's important that you get experience with things like this."

After he hung up his phone, he opened his eyes to find Melanie had followed him into the kitchen and stood frowning at him. "You're leaving already?"

"Can't be helped. I have a patient who's having a difficult labor." He held up his hands. "This only goes to show why I don't get involved in relationships. I can't always be there for things like family gatherings."

"Or helping me at my store tonight?"

He winced, remembering how he'd promised to help her. "I'll be there as soon as I'm able to."

"Thanks. I hope the mama and her pups are okay." She gave his shoulder a quick squeeze. He found his coat in the pile on his cousin's bed and went back to the dining room. He stood behind his mom, putting his hands on her shoulders. "I hate to eat and run, but I have a patient who really needs me."

Penny rose to her feet. "I'll make you a plate of leftovers to take with you for later."

He waved off her offer. "I appreciate the

offer, but I need to leave right now." He bent down and kissed his mother on the cheek. "I'll call you later." He turned to his family. "And happy Thanksgiving, everyone. I'll see you all soon."

He left the house and had almost made it to his car when his mom called his name. "Sorry, Mom. I've got to go."

She held out a foil-wrapped paper plate. "You can't leave without some pie."

He accepted the plate, then gave her a quick hug. "I wish I could stay. This is the second year in a row that I'll miss out on watching Aunt Sarah beat everyone at euchre."

"You mean me beating everyone at cards."

Jack smiled at that since his mom was notoriously bad at remembering which was trump suit. He got into his car and pulled away from the curb, holding his hand up in farewell.

"THERE'S GOT TO be a short or something in this string of lights," Mel muttered to the dog as she checked each bulb to make sure it was secure in the socket. She'd been at her bookstore since leaving Thanksgiving dinner at Penny and Christopher's house. She was anxious to start decorating before the shoppers descended on her the next day for Black Friday shopping. It would be the beginning of an incredibly busy month that left no extra time for things like running out of tinsel and burned-out bulbs.

In the last two hours, she had put up most of the decorations and had started on the Christmas tree, but the lights refused to work. Groaning in frustration, she rose to her feet and walked away from the lights and to the coffee counter to make a latte. She'd need the caffeine if she was going to be there all night at the rate this was going.

While she waited for the espresso to drip into her mug, she hummed along with the radio station that had been playing Christmas songs 24/7 since Halloween. She had started steaming the milk when she heard a knock on the front door. The dog rose to his feet and walked to the door, his tail wagging enthusiastically. Since she couldn't pause the steam, she let it continue but turned her head and tried to see who was standing there. Jack was at the front window, peering in with his hand resting along the top of his eyebrows. She held up one finger to let him know it would be a moment.

Once the milk was steamed and poured into her espresso, she walked to the front door to open it. "You made it," she said to Jack. She'd missed him after he'd left for the clinic. The family dinner wasn't the same without him there. She'd been paired with Josh's dad during the euchre tournament and came in a respectable second place behind Aunt Sarah and Mr. Duffy.

"Better late than never." He glanced around the store and whistled at her progress as he petted the dog's head. "Looks like you've been busy." He crouched down to look the dog in the eyes. "Were you a helper? Yes, you were. You're a good dog."

"Now if I could only get all the lights to work, my evening would be complete." She pointed at the string of bulbs in the middle of the tree that remained dark. "I've been checking each light, but I can't find the loose connection."

"Good thing that I'm here then." He took off his coat and draped it on a stool at the coffee bar before approaching the tree. He rubbed his hands together before kneeling in front of the tree and starting to check the connections.

She watched him for a moment. "Need some coffee?"

He turned to look at her, then focused on the lights. "That would be great. I'm heading back to the clinic after I help you here."

Mel went and put a cup under the coffee maker before pressing the button to begin brewing. She leaned on the counter, her eye on Jack. "How are things at the clinic? You didn't have to leave on my account. I feel bad. I would have been fine decorating on my own."

"I made you a promise, so I'm here. I don't break my plans with you."

"How is your patient?"

"Winnie's on the older side to be a first-time mother, but I think she'll be okay. And her puppies are healthy. And completely adorable."

"How many puppies?"

Jack turned to her, grinning. "Why? Interested in one?"

Mel wagged a finger at him. "No way,

mister vet, I have no room. I'm not home that much and..." She pushed off the counter and checked on the progress of the coffee. "Besides, I've decided to keep Dickens."

Jack paused with the lights to turn to look at her. "Dickens? You finally named him."

Mel motioned to the dog. "What can I say? He's grown on me. You win, or maybe I'm the winner. Anyway, I'm adopting a pet."

"I think you'll find the experience to be a very rewarding one. For both of you." Jack glanced around the room. "Who knows? Maybe he'll become the store mascot."

Jack leaned down again, studying the cord and fiddling with the bulbs. The lights on the tree flickered a few times before staying on. Mel clapped her hands. "You fixed them."

Jack rose to his feet and looked at the tree while Mel walked around the counter and handed him his fresh cup of coffee. "I'm good for some things at least." He glanced at the boxes that surrounded the tree. "Ready to put on ornaments?"

For the next half hour, they decorated the tree as old-time crooners like Bing Crosby and Perry Como serenaded them from the radio. Her ornaments for the store were those she'd found over the years that were literary themed. Settings, iconic items and fictional characters seemed to smile from their respective ornaments and approve of the holiday display as familiar carols wound their Christmas magic around the scene. She could imagine turning out the fluorescent lights in the store so that only the tree lights lit up the room while she and Jack stood with their arms around each other. Maybe even shared a kiss. It would have been a picture-perfect Christmas movie moment if it had started to snow outside.

But Jack didn't return her feelings. And she was working very hard to get over him.

"Mel, you didn't hear a thing I asked, did you?"

She felt her cheeks warm, caught in her thoughts. "No, I didn't. I was thinking of something else. What were you saying?"

"I asked where you put the tinsel from last year." He held up a box and turned it upside down, revealing it to be empty. "It's not in the box you labeled."

"I threw it out. It makes too big of a mess that trails around the store, then clogs up my vacuum." She stood back and observed the tree. "This is perfect like it is."

"But you've got to have tinsel. It's tradition."

She gave a shrug. "Maybe I'm trying new traditions this year."

"Is this part of your makeover too?"

"No, this is moving on from parts of my life that don't seem to be working."

Jack frowned at her, then placed the box on the counter before approaching her. "Are you okay? You seem a little down tonight."

She released a deep breath, letting the thoughts that she'd been keeping to herself come out. "It's the start of the holiday season, and I'm single and alone again. I thought that it would be different this year, but I seem to be stuck in a place that I can't get out of." She shook her head as if the thoughts would erase from her mind. Brooding about how alone she was wouldn't change anything. This was the time for action. For doing what she needed to in order to go after what she wanted.

She looked over at Jack. It was definitely time to move on. Time to stop using the makeover to get Jack's attention and instead focus on herself. Her life. Her happiness.

Because continuing to pine over Jack wasn't helping.

JACK HELPED MELANIE stack the empty decoration boxes in the storeroom. She seemed to be lost in thought, and he wanted to fix whatever it was that was bothering her. He put a hand on her shoulder after she placed the last box on the shelf. When she turned, he noticed that her eyelashes were damp. "What's wrong?"

She tried to grin. "It's been a long day. Let's just leave and go home."

He put his hands on either side of her face. "I don't like to see you so upset. Talk to me."

She put her hands on his and stared at him. "Talking's not going to help. Only doing."

"And what do you want to do?"

Her eyes seemed dim, the golden light in them fading as she stared into his. "I want to stop hurting. I want to start living. But it's hard to let go of what I'd hoped for for so long."

He knew she was talking about him. And he'd tried to see if he could reciprocate her feelings. To feel what Christopher had seemed to think he did. But then his job had gotten in the way again of pursuing a relationship. The emergency call had only proven what he already knew. His career would always be first, and he couldn't deny it. If he hadn't promised Mel that he'd help her ready the store for the holiday, he'd have spent the entire night at the clinic, watching over Winnie and her babies.

Jack rubbed his thumb over her cheek where a tear had tracked. "If I could change for you, I would. If I could love you like you need me to, I'd move heaven and earth to make it happen."

Mel gave a small nod, and he couldn't seem to say anything else.

When Mel left the storeroom, he knew that it was the last time she'd talk about a future with him. He sensed that she had made up her mind, and there was no going back. She would go back to their easy friendship without wondering what if.

Later as he settled on the floor next to Winnie, he replayed the moment in the storeroom.

Why did Mel stay in his mind after he left the store? What if he could love her like she wanted him to? What if the friendship they had always had wasn't the white-hot passion like he had with Stacey but a different, quiet kind of love that would complete the both of them? He could never be the man she needed. Could he love her like she wanted him to?

He put a hand on Winnie's head and gave her a soft pat before leaning his head back against the wall and closing his eyes.

CHAPTER EIGHT

MEL RANG ANOTHER sale and handed the shopper his bag of books and receipt. "Thank you for coming in today. Have a wonderful holiday."

He nodded at her, then clutched the bag to his chest before leaving. Mel turned to Emma who manned the coffee machine, making lattes and hot chocolates as fast as she could. The line for drinks stretched only slightly farther than the one for the cash register. Black Friday would be as good a day for her store's bottom line as she had hoped.

She rang up the next customer's purchases, still contemplating her relationship with Jack. As she'd undressed and gotten ready for bed, she'd shed her fantasy about him. And when she'd risen this morning and prepared for the day, she had put on hope for a different future than the one she'd often imagined. She was finally and completely over Jack.

Or at least she hoped she was on the right path for that.

No longer was she going to wonder if the looks he gave her meant something. No more would she spend even a second planning on how she could change his view of her. From now on, she was going to focus on finding a man who was actually interested in her too. And then building a life with this Mr. Right that would exceed any hopes she'd ever harbored over Jack.

She handed the customer her bag and receipt, then waited as the next customer approached. Marius looked at her with a hangdog look that he probably thought was charming. Oh, who was she kidding? It did make her smile. "I haven't heard from you in a while. Is your family okay?"

"I know I owe you an explanation, and I was hoping we could talk about that privately." He raised his eyebrows. "Maybe over dinner tonight after you close?"

She considered him before nodding. "I'd really like that."

He winked at her before placing a stack

of books on the counter. "My nephew loved those books from his birthday so much that I decided to give books to all the little rug rats on my Christmas list."

She eyed the pile that teetered, threatening to spill over the wooden counter. "You must have a large family?"

"Two older brothers who are both married with kids. I found out yesterday that nephew or niece number nine will arrive next spring."

Melanie whistled at this as she started to ring up the books. She'd always longed to have a big family. Maybe it was because she'd been an only child. That is until the Cuthberts had invited her into their fold. She pushed that thought aside and focused instead on the man in front of her. "Then you have a very blessed family."

"That I do." He gave her his credit card to finalize the purchase. "What time do you close tonight?"

"Seven."

"I'll be here at a little before." He held up two fingers. "Scout's honor."

"I'm giving you a second chance, Marius. Don't mess this one up."

He winked at her as she handed him his bag. Mel kept her eyes on him as he left the bookstore before turning to the next customer. It would be both of their second chances.

JACK SENT MEL a quick text. He was asking her if she'd like to meet him at Shelby's house after the store closed. For years, the Cuthbert cousins had met the Friday evening after Thanksgiving to strategize for upcoming holiday activities for the family. They had to finalize the plans for the fundraiser, which was in two weeks. Schedule a night of caroling at the seniors' center and another at the children's ward of the hospital. And whatever else Shelby had come up with to help them celebrate the season.

Jack wanted to invite Mel since she was practically an honorary member. Besides, he'd hoped to talk to her before the next committee meeting. How had it come up so quickly? Where had the time gone? And why did the years seem to go faster the older he got?

Not wanting to reflect on that thought too closely, he put his cell phone away and returned to his office. It was a light day with easy checkup appointments since most pet owners were presumably busy with the season, out shopping maybe or visiting friends or family. Still, he had a handful of patients to see.

His cell phone chimed, and he was surprised to hear from Mel so quickly. Knowing how busy the bookstore had to be, he figured he wouldn't get a message back from her for hours.

Can't tonight. Date with Marius. Cross your fingers.

Jack swallowed at the disappointment her text rose in his throat. So she was giving the guy a second chance. Good for her.

Then why did the thought of her out with another man suddenly make his chest ache?

Had to be the holidays and all the sentimental feelings they brought. So what if he had started to wonder what a relationship with Mel would be like? No. Focus on the job and forget about Mel.

Which is what he reminded himself

again as he arrived at Shelby's condo. Josh answered the front door, and Jack handed him the bottle of white wine he'd picked up from the store around the corner from the clinic. Josh looked down at the wine label. "Shelby will appreciate this. She was just saying that she'd forgotten to get some today."

"That doesn't sound like her. She's always so prepared." In fact, that's why the family usually turned to her to plan their get-togethers. She knew what needed to be done and how to delegate those tasks to other family members, a skill she'd learned at their grandmother's knee. She was good at it which was partly what had made her such a strong candidate for mayor of their town. She'd ultimately lost the election but won in the end when she fell for her opponent, Josh, and vice versa.

Shelby brought out a plate of veggies and dip and placed it on the coffee table. "Penny called to say they are on their way, and Laurel is here already making dinner. Kristina has to work late, but she'll be by after the salon closes. That's all I could get to agree to come tonight." She looked behind Jack. "I thought you were bringing Mel with you."

"She's got a date." The words soured on his tongue. "With Marius."

Shelby's eyebrows rose at the name but she didn't say another word. Instead she took the bottle of wine from Josh and returned to the kitchen. Josh motioned to the couch, so Jack took a seat and helped himself to a broccoli spear and dipped it into the dill dressing. Laurel appeared with a plate that held a nut-studded ball of cheese and ring of crackers around it. "Shelby says you're making dinner. I didn't know you could cook."

"It's surprising the things you learn when you're in rehab. We all had to earn our keep while I was there, and my talents turned out to be in the kitchen." She gave a shrug. "Who knew? And now I'm starting cooking school in January. Maybe one day you'll be eating at my own restaurant."

"I look forward to it, Laurel." And he meant it. He'd seen the struggles his cousin had gone through and was pleased to see the progress she had made since. He glanced around the living room. "Where's Harper?"

"Spending the night at Penny's. She loves playing with Daisy and Eli over there. When Penny offered to have a sitter watch them all tonight, I couldn't turn her down."

She sliced some of the cheese ball and spread it on a cracker before handing it to him. "Looks like we're all getting what we want, and it's about time, don't you think?"

He took a bite of the cracker and nodded at her. He was proud of the work she'd put into finding sobriety. Penny and Christopher soon arrived, and they started the planning meeting while eating the hors d'oeuvres and drinking the wine he had brought. All except Shelby who said she wasn't in the mood for alcohol that evening.

Before Laurel served dinner, they hammered out the calendar of events. As the director of the seniors' home, Christopher confirmed the night they would carol for his residents. Penny verified that Thora's fire department was sponsoring the wreath sale in conjunction with the fundraiser. But

Shelby was outvoted on the issue of a craft sale. Jack looked over the calendar. "We're already stretched thin as it is, Shel. Maybe next year."

Jack felt confident in the time line for the fundraiser. Melanie had been on top of many of the details so far, and with her busy selling season starting would hand over the majority of the last-minute minutiae for him to complete. Shelby gave him an intent look. "You're going to be able to handle this, right? The family is depending on you."

"I've never let the family down before, so you can depend on me."

She bit the edge of her thumb. "Maybe I should step back in and handle it all again."

Josh took her hand in his. "Jack said he can take care of it, so you need to let him. Trust your cousins, right?"

She nodded before turning to Jack. "If you do run into a snag though, I can help. After all, Aunt Sarah and I ran a successful fundraiser last year. The best one in family history."

"And this will be just as valuable. Mel and I have it under control," Jack assured her.

Penny looked around the living room. "I expected Mel to be here tonight."

"She's on a date," Shelby said. "With Marius."

Christopher's eyes met Jack's. "And you're okay with that?"

Jack stood and walked to the pass-through where he found and opened the bottle of wine that Penny and Christopher had brought with them and refilled his glass. "Why wouldn't I be? We're just friends. Like we've been saying all along."

Even if he had started to consider what a future with Mel might look like. Thoughts about her as more than a friend had started to slip into his brain. Making him see her in a different light.

He took a sip from his glass, then held up the bottle. "Who wants a refill?"

THE WAITER LEFT the table with their orders, and Mel glanced around the restaurant. She usually kept to the local eateries in Thora, but Marius had driven them to a tapas restaurant in downtown Detroit. When they'd entered the restaurant, they'd been greeted by a white lit Christmas tree. Even their table had a small holly centerpiece surrounding a red-and-white-striped votive candle. Glad that she'd taken the time to run home and switch into another outfit on her lunch break, she straightened the front of the blouse that she had planned on wearing the night of their first date. Seeing Marius's reaction to her when he'd arrived at her store had made the extra effort worth it.

Marius stared at her from the other side of the table. "I'm glad you gave me this second chance."

"My pleasure. I hope everything's okay with your family. You mentioned an emergency when you canceled our date." She took a sip of her wine, telling herself to enjoy the atmosphere. Marius was certainly attentive and there were no moms or wedding plans in sight.

He gave a nod. "I'm the youngest son of three boys who were raised by a single mother. I've always thought that it was my responsibility to take care of her. And when she had a heart attack on the afternoon of our date, I couldn't leave her."

Mel set her glass on the table, then

reached her hand out to his. "Oh, Marius, I'm sorry. I never thought it was something so serious. Why didn't you say so earlier?"

He squeezed her fingers. "I'm not the type of man who takes dating or relationships lightly, but my mother and her health have to come first. I had to be sure that she was going to be okay. I hope you can understand that."

"Of course I do." Now she felt silly for even asking him to explain.

He moved his thumb over hers. "I would have been there that night. I wanted to be. And then I figured that I had really messed things up with you, so I stayed away." His eyes searched hers. "But I can't stay away anymore. I really like you, Melanie."

She removed her hand from his and had another sip of wine. "But you hardly know me."

"That's something I'm hoping we can change. That is if you're interested."

The waiter returned with their salads, and Marius's attention shifted. Grateful for a moment to calm her wildly beating heart, Melanie unrolled the cloth napkin to arrange her silverware beside the plate.

The words were nice to hear, and Marius seemed to be sincere. So why was she hesitating? Jack's face popped into her mind, and she quickly dismissed it. She was getting over him. And Marius was giving her an opportunity to do just that.

Resolved in her decision, she said, "I think that I'd like to get to know you better too."

Marius returned her smile. "Good. So tell me every single thing about you from the day you were born." They both laughed.

"That could take a while." She glanced at her watch. "How much time do you have?"

"I've got the rest of this evening… The rest of my life if you want it."

Over salads, she shared about losing her mom at a young age, and she learned that he'd never known his father who had died a few months before he was born. When their entrées arrived, she found out that his mother was a nurse who had set him on his path in the medical field while she told him about her strained relationship with her father. It was different talking to a man who didn't know every single thing that had happened to her from kindergarten on. She could share what she wanted and withhold what she didn't. Part of that was refreshing.

By the time dessert arrived, a chocolate mousse with two spoons for them to share, Melanie realized that she liked Marius. He was intelligent, kind and charming. He made her bubble with laughter with his stories as well as made her eyes mist with feeling. When he asked her out again, she agreed readily. He smiled at her eagerness and asked, "When?"

She thought about her upcoming busy schedule at the store, then shrugged it off. "Is tomorrow night too soon?"

He winced. "I would take you up on that, but I'm working night shift for a friend of mine. What about Sunday night?"

Jack intruded on her date once again. "I have a meeting for a fundraiser I'm cochairing. Monday?"

He reached across the table and took her hand in his. "I'll be counting down the minutes." He eyed her. "Ever been iceskating?"

They made plans to go skating in the park near Thora's city hall where a large ice rink had been set up through the New Year. And Melanie found herself looking forward to it.

AUNT SARAH SAT on the couch in her apartment as she listened to the update on the plans for the fundraiser, nodding at different times. When Mel finished with their report, his great-aunt clapped enthusiastically. "Very good. I knew things would work out with you two at the helm."

Jack peered at her, knowing the older woman had more to say. "But...?"

"But I think we need to do something a little different this year." She looked between him and Mel, then nodded. "I think it's time we added a little competition into the event."

Jack frowned and glanced at Mel who shrugged and looked confused. "Like who brings in the most money for the night?"

"Sort of." She crossed her arms and tapped one of her fingers on her lips. "You know my favorite show is the one where the dancers compete. Well, I read a newspaper article about this group of doctors who raise money for a charity by dancing with one of their patients and competing to see who raises the most money. People vote for their favorite couple by pledging money. The couple who raises the most money wins the competition."

Jack tried to close his mouth which gaped open. "And you think that Mel and I should add this to the fundraiser? Less than two weeks before it happens?"

"Of course. I've already talked to your cousins who have mostly agreed to participate."

Mostly. Jack could bet which ones had balked at the suggestion. Although he figured his sister, Michele, would jump at the chance to get Colin on the dance floor. "This would be a great idea to include in next year's fundraiser." Which he wouldn't be in charge of, thankfully. "It would give us more time to work this into the festivities."

"Ticket sales are down from where they were last year, Jack. We need something to boost our numbers."

Jack glanced at Mel. "I thought we were on track."

"Sales have slowed since we first released the tickets," she answered. "What could it hurt to do this now?"

He turned back to his aunt. "Fine. We'll add the dancing competition to raise more money, but I've got to confess I hope the others are good dancers because I'm not the lightest guy on his feet out on a dance floor."

Aunt Sarah smiled at him, a wicked gleam in her eye. Uh-oh. "That won't be a problem. You'll dance with Melanie. It's only fitting since you both are cohosting the event." His aunt turned to Mel. "Do you have a problem with that?"

"I don't know how to dance either."

Aunt Sarah's smile grew wider. "That's fine because I've signed you both up for a lesson with a friend of mine, Monsieur LeBlanc. He's expecting you two to be at his dance studio Wednesday night."

By the time he left his great-aunt's apartment, Jack felt as if his life had spiraled out of control with the help of a charming octogenarian. As he drove them back to

Mel's house, he glanced at her in the passenger seat. "Are you convinced we should do this?"

"I think it's a good idea to raise more money. People will like it."

He wasn't so sure. "Maybe I'll sprain my ankle between now and then and get out of it that way."

"Don't be such a spoilsport. I've always wanted to learn how to ballroom dance beyond doing the waltz." She darted her eyes to him. "You remember in fifth grade when the music teacher tried to teach us?"

"I remember Miss Rex asking me to stop stepping on all the girls' feet." He glanced at her again. "You look different tonight."

"I tried a new cosmetics technique with contouring that Kristina taught me."

"No, it's not the makeup." Although she did look beautiful. "Is it Marius? Have you talked to him since your date the other night?"

She smiled and glanced out the window. Jack knew that if the lights were on he'd see a blush on her cheeks. "Maybe. It was a good first date."

"Just good?"

She turned back to face him. "Okay, it was wonderful. Marius is a really nice guy."

Oh. "Are you planning on seeing him again?"

"We're going ice-skating tomorrow night in the park."

"Have you ever gone ice-skating?"

"No, but that doesn't mean I won't enjoy Marius teaching me." She touched her lips with her fingertips and smiled again.

He kept his gaze out the windshield until he reached Melanie's house. He started to get out of the car to walk her up to her porch, but she waved him back. "You don't have to get out with me. I'll see you Wednesday night for our first dance lesson?"

He tried to smile but couldn't find the energy. Instead, he watched as she ran up to her house and let herself inside, her phone ringing before she closed the door.

Closing his eyes, he realized that Mel had moved on. This is what he had wanted, right? For her to move on from her little crush on him and find a man who could love her the way she wanted.

So why did he dread what would happen Monday night on her next date?

MEL STOOD AND rubbed her backside that had just found contact with the hard icy surface of the rink. "I don't think I'm meant to be an ice-skater."

Marius put his arm around her shoulder. "You just need more practice. Come on. Let's go one more time around the rink, then I'll buy you a hot chocolate for a reward."

He put his hand in hers as they attempted another turn around the rink. Despite the times she'd fallen on the ice, she was enjoying herself. There was a nip in the air, but the physical effort of skating kept her warm. And the man next to her kept an eye on her, making her feel cherished.

Her ankle started to turn inward, and she groaned as she fell once again onto the ice. "Ooo, that one's going to leave a bruise. How do you stay on these tiny blades? You're a much bigger person than I am, but you have no problem staying up."

Marius held out his hand once again. "Years and years of playing hockey with my brothers." He helped raise her to her feet. "I think it's time for that hot chocolate."

"Extra whipped cream?"

"You've definitely earned it."

Slowly, they made their way to the edge of the ice. Mel started to wobble, but Marius pulled her tight to his side, holding her up with his arm around her waist. His touch felt good, and she wondered if he'd kiss her tonight. And would she welcome that kiss?

He held her tighter, and she knew she definitely would.

Once off the ice, they sat on a bench and removed their skates. Mel groaned as she took off the last one and massaged her ankle. "I'm sure not meant to enter an ice-skating competition anytime soon."

"I don't know. I think you have more grace than you give yourself credit for. After all, this was the first time you've been on the ice." He moved her hand aside and took over checking her ankle. "Your ankles might swell tonight. If they do, apply heat then cold compresses to ease the swelling."

She opened her eyes to look at his bowed head. For a moment, she wondered what Jack was doing but let the thought pass. Marius raised his eyes to hers, and he leaned forward to press his mouth against hers.

Her eyes fluttered shut, and she tried to lose herself in the kiss.

Marius backed away. "I've been wanting to do that since I met you on Halloween night."

She nodded, not quite sure what was wrong. The kiss was nice, but... She couldn't put her finger on it and opted to move past it.

"I believe I was promised hot chocolate."

He grinned, and they finished putting on their boots. They returned her skates to the rental booth, then walked over to the food truck that offered hot drinks and snacks. As they waited in the long line, Mel's thoughts drifted to the upcoming big holiday event. "Would it be too bold if I asked you to come to the fundraiser I'm cochairing a week from Friday?"

He turned to look at her. "I've been waiting for you to ask me since you told me about it."

"It's formal, and I'm hosting it along with my friend Jack."

"Ah, yes. This Jack you keep talking about." He peered at her. "Do I have anything to worry about when it comes to you and Jack?"

She shook her head. "No." At least, not anymore. She'd finally given up on that dream of him. "I told you. We're just friends. Actually, he's been my best friend since we were five years old. If anything were going to happen with him, it would have happened long before now." Besides, Jack kept reminding her that he didn't feel that way about her.

Marius put his arm around her shoulders as they took a few steps forward in the line. "Good. Because I want you all to myself." He looked at her then. "Are you okay with that?"

She opened her mouth to answer, then shut it just as quickly. What did she want when it came to Marius? Was he asking her to date him exclusively? Instead of answering him, she examined the menu printed on the large blackboard easel. "Oooh, they have gingerbread cookies. My mom and I used to make them every Christmas when I was little."

"Then you shall have one tonight."

They got their cups of hot chocolate, extra whipped cream on Mel's, as well as gingerbread cookies and stood at one of the tall tables that dotted the edge of the ice rink. Mel bit into her cookie and closed her eyes. It didn't taste exactly like the cookies she'd made with her mother, but it reminded her of them. "Good?" Marius asked.

She opened her eyes and nodded. "Close enough."

She sipped her drink, appreciating how it went down her throat and warmed her from the inside out.

"I've told my mother about you."

Mel raised an eyebrow at this. "So soon?"

He shrugged. "To be honest, I told her about you the night we met at your store. Told her that I met a woman I could fall in love with."

"Marius—"

"I know. I'm rushing things. But I know what I want, and that's you." He peered at her and reached out to touch her hand. "What about you?"

She considered his words. She knew that she didn't want to be alone for the holidays, and Marius was offering the chance to be with him. That he could offer her a future that Jack couldn't. And wasn't the point of her makeover and the changes in her life about imagining a different life than the one she'd been leading?

She knew that Marius would be good for her. That he could step easily into the empty space in her life.

Snowflakes started drifting down. Marius laughed as he tipped his head back, opening his mouth to catch a few flakes on his tongue.

He could make her happy.

She stepped around the table and put her hands on his shoulders. He turned his gaze to hers. "I think that this is going to be an amazing Christmas for us both."

He dipped his head to kiss her, and she tried to make it be enough for her.

MEL GLANCED DOWN at the skirt she wore. Shelby had told her to wear it for the dance lesson along with a loose top. She should know. She and Josh had also taken a dance lesson the night before to prepare for the fundraiser as well, and had given her advice about what to expect. "It's going to feel weird and uncomfortable at first, but I'm sure you and Jack will get the hang of it pretty quickly. You're both so athletic."

Mel doubted that her history on the track team in high school would translate to grace on the dance floor. It certainly hadn't on the ice. She put her hands on her cheeks and shook her head at the memory. She'd spent more time falling than skating. But Marius had been encouraging and sweet. And they'd made plans to go out later that week.

This time with Marius had been worlds better than her experiences last month with dating. No mother in sight. No talk of trying to sell her insurance. And he paid attention to her as she talked about silly things like how her espresso machine had spurted steamed milk all down her sweater the other morning when she'd been making a latte for a customer. Or more serious topics like how she worried that Shelby's new marriage would affect their relationship over time. He listened and offered advice when she asked.

The dance instructor smiled as he approached Mel. "Your partner is late?"

"He had a last-minute surgery, but he'll be here as soon as he can."

"Then I will dance with you until he is." The instructor put on some music, then turned to her. "What dance experience do you have?"

"None, I'm afraid. Unless you count swaying side to side at school dances and weddings."

The front door of the dance studio opened, and Jack rushed in, bringing in a chill from outside. "Sorry I'm late. But the good news is that the collie is going to be just fine."

The dance instructor frowned at him and looked up at the clock on the wall. "I have less than ninety minutes to teach you the rumba." He looked Jack over from head to foot. "And I can tell that I'm going to need every one of them with you."

For the next hour, the instructor danced with each of them, showing them how to move to the music. The last half hour, he finally put Jack and Mel together. She hoped that she could remember his instructions. Sway her hips. Connect her eyes to Jack's. Follow his lead.

The music began, and Mel found herself plastered against Jack who winced as he stepped on her foot. "Sorry."

She shook off the apology. "We're still learning."

"Again," the instructor called as he started over the music from the beginning.

Mel looked into Jack's eyes as he put his hands on her waist and brought her closer to him. The space seemed to heat between them as they swayed to the music before he stepped behind her and ran his hand up her waist.

Biting her lip to stop the confusion that seemed to rise at his touch, she concentrated instead on the steps. Until he stepped on her foot again.

Jack let go of her and hung his head. "I told you that I'm no good at this."

"You're doing okay." She put a hand on his bicep. "Don't be so hard on yourself. This isn't easy for either one of us. We'll do fine."

He raised his eyes to look at her. "We're not going to make much money if we're just fine. I want to win, don't you? Maybe hold this over my sister a little?"

"We have just over a week. How good do you think we're going to get in such a short space of time?" She shook her head. "Right now, I'm trying to not embarrass either one of us. I'm not looking for great dance moves."

"Let's face it. We're going to need to practice often." He turned to Monsieur LeBlanc. "How much do you charge for extra lessons?"

"Mademoiselle is right. You don't have the talent for this."

Jack put his hands on his hips. "How much for another hour tonight?" He turned to Mel. "Unless you have another date tonight."

"Not until Friday."

Jack turned back to the instructor. "How much?"

JACK WOULDN'T FAULT the dance instructor if he never gave him another dance lesson. He was hopeless when it came to this, but he was also determined that he wouldn't let himself, his aunt or Mel down.

But more than that, it was holding Mel in his arms for another hour. He might step on her foot but when she was so close to him, he forgot the next steps. He closed his eyes and bent at the waist, letting out a breath of frustration.

"You're trying too hard," Monsieur LeBlanc said in a soft accented voice.

Jack straightened and looked across the room at Mel who practiced her part of the dance while watching herself in the mirror. "I don't know what else to do. I want to win."

"The dance or the girl?"

He looked at Monsieur. "The dance, of course. I feel like I can do this."

The instructor nodded and put on the song they'd been assigned to dance to. Melanie drew near him and put her hands on his shoulders. At the musical cue, he dipped her slowly, then brought her up so that she faced him.

By the time the hour passed, Jack was no closer to being more graceful but at least he knew the dance. Executing it, on the other hand, was far from successful. The last run-through, he had tripped over his own foot and landed on the floor, pulling Mel down on top of him. She'd giggled at it, and eventually, he'd joined in. Monsieur merely huffed and looked away.

He stood and helped her to her feet. She smiled into his face. "You've got to admit that was funny. Stop being so worried about hurting me because I don't think you could do any more harm than you already have."

He liked her teasing, it meant they truly were friends again. "I'm never going to get this dance." He strode to the other end of the room where their things waited. Pulling out his wallet, he took out the agreed upon amount for the extra hour, then handed it to Monsieur LeBlanc.

As he tugged on his coat, Mel watched him, her head cocked to one side. "You need to lighten up. Maybe that's why you're so stiff when we're dancing."

Maybe. But holding Mel had only confused him even more than he was. She was his best friend, he kept reminding himself. Not his girlfriend. But his heart had reacted to her nearness as if there was more than friendship.

He groaned and stared up at the ceiling. He needed to get this in check. To stop thinking about Mel like that. She was obviously taken with this other guy. His chance with her had passed before he realized that he was interested in her. He took a deep breath to calm his emotions, then looked over at her. "I'm going to need more practice. Are you free tomorrow after work? I can move the furniture in my living room to give us the space to dance."

She nodded and studied him. "It's more than the dance that's upsetting you." She stepped closer to him, and he could smell the perfume she'd put on that morning. "What's going on, Jack?"

"Nothing." He couldn't tell her about this. Not when she seemed so happy with Marius. Besides, he was going to be busy with the fundraiser and the clinic in the next few weeks. Now wasn't the right time to approach her.

"I know when you're going through stuff, so don't think you can lie to me and get away with it. What's up?"

He couldn't exactly tell her that he was confused about her. And all of it. That nothing seemed to be working in his life anymore. That her admission about her feelings for him on Halloween had started a chain reaction in him that made him realize that he wasn't as content with his life as he had once thought he was. That he had started to wonder what if there was more to life than what he had. What if he pursued her formally, officially? What if he tried kissing her like he meant it rather than trying to keep her at arm's length?

Instead, he shook his head again. "It's nothing. Work stuff." He paused. "Are you interested in adopting a kitten? I have one that's missing an ear, but he's in good health otherwise. Bit of a fighter with the other cats, but loves to snuggle with humans. He'd be great in a one pet family."

"I told you, Jack. I've got my hands full with Dickens. You might have convinced me that he's a good fit for me, but I can't take on another pet." She touched the tip of his nose with her finger. "Even you can't change my mind about that."

"I'll wear you down yet."

She laughed at that, and he followed her outside the studio, wondering what he was going to do with these inconvenient feelings that had arisen.

CHAPTER NINE

JACK STOOD IN his office, moving his feet according to the steps of the dance that he'd been taught by Monsieur LeBlanc. When his office door opened, he stopped and closed his eyes, wondering who had caught him practicing. Turning, he found Shelby watching him with an amused grin. "Don't let me stop you. It looked pretty good."

"Mel makes me look better." Curious, he asked, "What are you doing here? Picking out one of my rescue dogs for you and Josh? Or maybe a feline companion for your father-in-law?"

"We can talk pets next year once we're settled into a new place. I actually came to invite you to lunch. My treat. Have you eaten?"

He hadn't remembered to eat breakfast, and his stomach growled in protest at the slip. Glancing at his watch, he grimaced. "I would, but I have an appointment in ten minutes. Rain check?"

"Sure." She entered the office and took a seat on the edge of his desk. "How are the dance lessons going?"

He groaned at the thought. He'd been spending every spare minute of his schedule rehearsing the steps, but he didn't seem to be making a lot of progress. "You saw how I'm doing. I'm hopeless."

"Not hopeless. Just uncoordinated."

It seemed like the same thing to him. "Why is Aunt Sarah making us do this? Isn't it enough that we put on a huge event every year? Now she has to add competitive ballroom dancing to the mix?" He groaned and ran a hand over his face. "How are you and Josh doing on your dance?"

"A little better than you from the looks of it. Bert watches us and gives tips that he's learned from watching dancing competition shows on television over the years. Very helpful."

"I bet." Jack remembered how Bert had been critical of the high school football team and had yelled coaching advice from the bleachers. "So what's the real reason you showed up at my office? What were you going to ask me over lunch?"

"Am I that obvious?"

"Since you don't have a pet, the only time I see you at the clinic is when you're about to ask for a favor. So what is it?"

She waved him off. "It can wait."

Jack watched her as she squirmed on the edge of the desk before she pushed off and started to pace around the office, glancing at him before asking, "Who takes care of the accounting for your clinic?"

He'd been expecting this conversation since she had mentioned that she was going to open her own accounting business. "It's mostly me trying to figure out everything at the end of the day. I hire someone at tax time, but other than that I do okay muddling through the accounts on a daily basis."

She stopped walking and turned to look at him. "And your clients are paying on time?"

"For the most part. I don't know. I lose track sometimes."

She smiled as if he'd said something brilliant. "That's why you need to hire me. I can take care of your books, and you can focus on your animals."

He nodded slowly. "So you were going to butter me up with lunch and offer your services? I was already planning on hiring you. All you had to do was ask me."

"Good." She looked him over. "You're not sleeping. What's going on?"

"Who says I'm not sleeping?"

She pointed at his face. "The dark circles under your eyes. Staying up late with patients?"

He paused, wondering if he could bring up his confusion over Mel. "Has Mel told you about her dates with Marius?"

Shelby nodded, grinning from ear to ear. "Of course. I think she likes him. And from what she's said, he feels the same way about her." She stopped and looked at him. "You said that you're not interested in dating her yourself, so what's the problem?"

It was as he suspected. "It's nothing. It's just…confusing when I'm dancing with her. We're close and touching and…" He ran a hand over his face. "I didn't think

I had those feelings for her, but now I'm wondering why I can't stop thinking about her."

Shelby sighed and shook her head at him. "Jack, I love you, but you're so clueless."

"Meaning?"

"You've always had these feelings, but you've been in denial so long that you haven't recognized them until now." She crossed her arms and peered at him. "But you're too late, unfortunately. She's moved on with Marius. Don't you dare mess that up for her."

"You think I don't know that I missed my chance with her? That's what is keeping me awake at night." He groaned. "I've been an idiot."

"No argument from me on that one."

She might have softened the blow a little, but he knew she was right. Whatever chance he might have had with Mel had passed. "So what am I supposed to do now?"

Shelby walked toward him and put a hand on his arm. "You do what Mel has done for years. You keep this to yourself because her happiness is more important to you."

He nodded and dropped his gaze to the floor. "I know you're right."

"I'm sorry, Jack. We tried to warn you that your chance with her was about to end. But you stubbornly believed that you didn't love her."

He brought his eyes back up to meet his cousin's. "I've always loved her. That wasn't the issue. I just assumed that I didn't have romantic feelings for her. We didn't have those kinds of fireworks between us."

"So what's different? The fact that she's with someone else now?"

"No, it's not about Marius." That would make him someone who would toy with Mel's feelings for his own gain. He wouldn't ever do that to her. "It's just different. I'm seeing her through different eyes."

"She gets a haircut and a new wardrobe, and that's all it took for you to notice her?"

"It isn't about how she looks." He paused and closed his eyes, shaking his head, knowing that he wasn't being very clear about how he was feeling. "I'm saying this all wrong, but I don't know how to describe what's changed between us. Maybe because she brought it out into the open when she confessed her feelings for me. I don't know." He straightened a stack of papers on his desk. "Besides, it doesn't matter. She's with Marius, and I have to accept it."

Lucas knocked on the office door as he opened it. "Your next appointment is here. And I'm heading to lunch."

Jack looked over at Shelby. "Seems like our time is up today."

"We can talk later?"

He put on his white lab coat. "There's nothing more to say. Because you're right. I lost my chance with Mel, and she's moved on. Just like I should do the same."

"Just make sure you don't hurt Mel, or yourself."

"You don't have to worry about that." He'd learned that the hard way already.

MEL RUBBED HER shin as she sat on Jack's couch. "That move definitely needs more practice."

"I feel like I should get a T-shirt printed with 'I'm sorry' on it so I don't have to keep saying the words." He knelt down and moved her hands aside. "I hope I didn't leave a bruise."

She ignored the frisson of pleasure at being this close to Jack. It reminded her of Marius and the ice rink. She closed her eyes to remind herself that she was dating the other man and not Jack. But then what could a few more seconds hurt?

Jack stood. "I've been practicing at the clinic every spare second that I have. Do you know how hard it is to flea dip a cat who doesn't want one?" He held up his arm where dark red scratches marked him. "Snowball let me know that she wasn't interested with her claws."

"Poor baby." She ran a finger down one of the scratches, and Jack gasped at her touch and flinched. "Did that hurt you?"

He shook his head and stepped away from her. "Do you want to try that sequence again?"

"I need a break." She ran a hand along the back of her neck to let some air get to the damp tendrils that clung there. "Dancing is more of a workout than my spin class."

"Agreed. I thought I was in shape until we started this, but I'm discovering muscle aches that I never knew before."

She eyed him and disagreed mentally with that statement. He'd always been in good shape. She rose to her feet and followed him to the kitchen. "Have you found a date for the fundraiser yet?"

He winced. "I'm debating about going stag. It wouldn't be fair to my date with all the duties that evening." He got a glass of water for himself and offered her one. "You taking Marius?"

"I asked him the other night, but you're right. We'll be so busy that he'll probably spend most of the evening alone. I should have thought of that."

"Things are going well with him then?"

She dropped her gaze to the carpet and smiled, biting her lip. Things were going really well with Marius, but she couldn't tell Jack that, could she? He'd insisted that they were just friends this whole time, but sharing those details with him felt awkward. "They're good," she replied. Jack nodded, his lips pursed as if he'd bit into a lemon. She frowned. "What's that look for?"

"What look?"

He grimaced again, and she pointed at him. "That look. What's wrong with Marius?"

"I don't know him well enough to say if there's something wrong."

She peered at him, wondering what Jack was thinking. "Are you asking me to introduce you two?"

He shrugged. "You're my best friend, and you haven't let me meet him? And you've been on what? Three dates now? Don't you think it's time?"

The thought of Marius and Jack getting acquainted made Mel pause. Did she really want that? True, Marius had just texted her about that very thing the other day, but she didn't know if she was ready for the two of them to meet. "I'm not sure that's a good idea."

"Why not? Do you think I'm not going to like him when you obviously do?"

"It's not just that." She took a seat on the sofa again and tried to sort through the feelings Jack's request had brought up in her mind. If Jack didn't like him, then it would become awkward if things progressed with Marius. She'd be caught between her best friend and boyfriend, not a great situation for any of them. "I…" She sighed. "It's too soon. We only started dating a week ago."

"And you're afraid of my opinion of him."

"No." *Yes*.

"We can make it a group thing with Shelby and Penny if you would prefer. Better to introduce him to the family in small groups."

"They're your family, not mine."

Jack frowned at her words, and he stared at her. "They're your family too. You may not have been born into it, but you're just as much a Cuthbert as I am."

She looked down at her hands. There wasn't any way to get out of this, was there? She finally nodded. "I'll talk to him. See if he wants to." Though she knew he would.

Jack came to stand next to her. "And you should bring him to the fundraiser. If he's going to be a big part of your life, then he should be included in what you're involved in. I would want to be if I was him."

She looked up into Jack's eyes and could see the sincerity there. "You don't think it would be awkward having him there while the two of us are dancing together?"

"Why not? It's not like you and I are really together. We're just dancing."

So why did she feel as if Jack meeting Marius was bound to be a disaster?

"I'll talk to him."

THEY SHOULD CALL themselves the Cuthbert Family Singers and take their act on the road, Jack surmised as he sang another Christmas carol with his cousins and their families at the seniors' home. He reached up to adjust the scratchy Santa hat that Penny had placed on his head before the singing began. As the song ended, Shelby played a flourish on the piano and turned on the bench to smile at their audience, a collection of senior citizens who smiled and clapped in response.

"Any other requests?" Shelby asked.

Mr. Duffy held up a finger. "I've always

been partial to 'I'll Be Home for Christmas.'"

Shelby nodded, and they shuffled through the stack of pages that had been copied for each of them. Mel, standing next to him, nudged him as a tall younger man joined the audience near the back of the room. "He's here."

Jack looked the man over. "That's Marius?"

"I told him we were singing here tonight and suggested he join us, but I didn't expect him to take the time to actually show up."

As the next song began, Jack watched Marius listen to their group singing. He looked tall and lean, but built, in the sweater and jeans that he wore. Clean-shaven compared to Jack's beard. His hair cropped close to his head. He didn't look like any nurse that Jack had ever known. More like a former football star who would sweep in and take Mel away from him.

Not take away. He had to keep telling himself that Marius would add to Mel's life in a way that he couldn't. He wanted only what was best for his dearest friend.

He glanced at Mel who blushed as she kept her gaze on Marius, grinning through the words of the song. She was definitely smitten. Good for her. She deserved a man who would make her smile. Love her the way she deserved. He squelched a protest from his heart that he should be that person for Mel and concentrated on singing the lyrics.

The song concluded, and so did the concert. Jack took the hat off his head and handed it back to Shelby who looked over his shoulder. "Marius is here."

"I saw."

"We should go meet him, don't you think?"

She started to walk toward the couple, but he stayed her with a touch of his hand on her arm. "Give them space. Mel will introduce him to us when she's ready."

Shelby turned her gaze back to his. "Will you be okay with that?"

He glanced over at Mel talking to Marius, a big smile on her face. How he wished he could have been the one to put it there. "I have to be, don't I?"

She squealed as Josh pulled her into an embrace and buried his face into her neck. "We have an audience," she told him as he kissed her.

"So let them see how much I am in love with my wife." He kissed her neck, then turned to Jack. "You ready for the dance competition? Because I should warn you. Shel and I are fantastic."

"You talking trash already? Because Christopher and I are going to win that thing." Penny waved at her husband who was helping an elderly man settle back into his wheelchair. Christopher smiled and waved back. "We're doing a tango that will make you cry it's so good."

Mel cleared her throat before she joined the group, holding Marius's hand in hers. "Hey, guys. I want to introduce you all to Marius."

The man in question thrust out his hand to Jack first. "So, this is Jack. Mel's told me a lot about you."

"All good, I hope."

Marius exchanged looks with Mel who smiled. "It was all good." What else could she say?

Jack returned the smile but his inner toddler pouted and crossed his arms. He wanted to like the guy since Mel was so wild about him, but his own feelings for her warred with that wish. Resisting the urge to nitpick all the things he didn't like about the man, he focused instead on how he spoke with the other cousins and their partners. Polite and respectful, he even laughed when Penny commented about his physique. "Maybe you could work out with Christopher and give him pointers."

Christopher nudged his wife. "I'm standing right here. No need to slobber over the new guy." He thrust out his hand. "Nice to meet you. And I'd be willing to trade workout tips for pointers on how to get along with this family."

Marius turned to Mel, frowning. "I thought you said you didn't have any family in the area."

Shelby put an arm around Mel's shoulders. "She may not officially be a Cuthbert, but we've practically adopted her."

After all the introductions were made, the group dispersed, some to go caroling through the seniors' home while others lingered in the lobby, talking and discussing the upcoming fundraiser. Mel and Marius stood close to each other, smiling into each other's faces. Jack swallowed at the lump that had lodged in the back of his throat. Marius turned to him and waved him over. "Mel and I were talking about going out for some dessert after this. Interested in joining us? I'd really like to get to know her best friend better."

Mel's eyes searched his, and Jack found himself turning down the invitation. He could be courteous and gracious, but he wasn't quite ready for this. He needed some more time to put his feelings for Mel in a locked box where they wouldn't escape. "I have an early surgery tomorrow morning. But I'll be seeing you both at the fundraiser Friday night?"

Marius nodded. "Mel told me all about this big shindig the two of you have been planning. And I can't wait to see the dance. From what she tells me, it's going to be a great show."

Jack smiled and nodded to Mel. "We're

still meeting tomorrow night for practice
and last-minute plans?"

"I'll be there."

He left the happy couple, well…happy.

CHAPTER TEN

MELANIE HAD LEFT the bookstore in her capable assistant's hands for the day so that she could spend it getting ready for the fundraiser to be held that evening. She'd been at the rental hall since seven with Shelby decorating and coordinating the deliveries of toys, flowers and all the various last-minute details required by such an event. Yawning, she covered her mouth. "I think I need another coffee."

"The first urn wasn't enough for you?" Shelby asked as she placed a holly centerpiece in the middle of a table covered by a red cloth. "Didn't you get much sleep last night? I told you today would be a marathon, not a sprint, so you needed to get plenty of rest."

"Marius and I stayed up talking until after midnight when I finally kicked him out so I could get some sleep."

Shelby's eyebrows rose at this. "Talking is good. What were you discussing so late?"

"Plans for Christmas. He wants me to go with him to his mother's house on Christmas Eve."

"Meeting the family already?" Shelby whistled. "Things must be going really well between the two of you."

They were going well, but she wasn't sure she was ready to take such a significant step in their relationship. Which is what they'd been arguing about so late. No, not arguing. Discussing rationally. She stifled another yawn. "I guess so."

Shelby stopped fluffing the greenery to peer at Melanie. "What's to guess? If he's introducing you to his mother, then I'd say he's pretty serious about you. Question is, are you just as serious about him?"

Mel walked to the next table rather than answer the question. While she had stayed up late talking with Marius, it was doubts and questions that had made her toss and turn the rest of the night. Things were moving way too fast for her comfort, but then wasn't that the point of her putting herself out there? She took another wreath and placed it in the center of the table, then added the red pillar candle in the middle.

Shelby walked to the table and waved with a flourish. "Earth to Mel, did you hear what I asked?"

"I heard, but I don't know how to answer that. I'm not sure how I feel about Marius."

"A nice, good-looking man is interested in you. He makes you happy. What is there not to be sure about?" Shelby stopped. "Don't tell me this is about Jack."

Mel raised her eyes to her friend's and gave a one-shoulder shrug. "Maybe?" When Shelby looked confused, Mel reacted. "I've loved Jack for so long. Maybe I don't know how to turn on those feelings for another man."

"It's not about turning on your feelings. It's about letting the relationship between the two of you develop and grow stronger. That is what you want, isn't it?"

Mel nodded. "I do."

"Then what are you so afraid of?"

She took a seat at the table, and Shelby took the one beside it. "I don't know. I should be thrilled that Marius is so interested in me. So why am I hesitating? When I'm with him, I'm happy and think that it's right for me. It's when I'm by myself that I have these doubts."

"Have you told Marius about them?"

"I can't tell him that I'm not sure about our relationship."

"Why not? Maybe he's as insecure as you are."

Mel picked at a piece of lint on the tablecloth. "I'm afraid that we're getting too serious too soon. It's only been two weeks, but he's talking about dating exclusively, and me meeting his family and going on a trip together next summer. And maybe moving in together eventually?"

Shelby whistled. "Have you asked him to slow things down a little?"

Mel shook her head. "I really like him. I do."

"But…?"

"But it's too soon."

Shelby put her hand on Mel's, clasping it. "You've loved Jack for over twenty-five years. It's going to take a little longer than two weeks to get over him and move on with a new guy."

"But that's just it. It's not only my feelings for Jack that are keeping me from moving forward with Marius."

"Then what else is?"

Now it was Mel's turn to be confused. "I haven't figured that part out yet."

"If you're not ready to move this fast with Marius, be up front with him and tell him. And if you're not ready to be exclusive with him, tell him that as well."

"It's not like I have a lot of other options waiting for me." She wasn't interested in dating anyone else right now as it was, but the idea of being exclusive with Marius gave her pause.

Shelby looked her over, then dropped her glance to the tablecloth. "I wouldn't be so sure about that. There might be someone else."

She stood then, and Mel followed her to the next table. "Who? What are you talking about?"

Shelby tried to look preoccupied and placed the next wreath on the table. "Nothing." She arranged the greenery, then the candle in the center before turning to Mel. "But if you're not ready, you don't have to get serious with Marius so soon. Ask for space. More time. And don't close yourself off to other opportunities that might arise."

"You're talking in code. What other opportunities do you mean?"

Shelby glanced at her, and Mel could see that she was keeping something back from her. Her friend pursed her lips. "Maybe you need to talk to Jack."

"Why would I need to talk to him about Marius? What does he have to do with this? They seemed to like each other when he met you all the other night."

Shelby opened her mouth, then closed it. "Forget I said anything. Let's finish decorating so we can go home and get ready."

"If there's something I need to know, you have to tell me." She put her hand on Shelby's arm. "What's going on?"

"Nothing. Nothing's going on. Keep your focus on tonight."

The catering manager walked out from the kitchen with her clipboard in hand and approached them. "Are we able to finalize the time line for this evening?"

Mel snuck a peek at Shelby who seemed relieved for the distraction. Something was going on, but the fundraiser had to take priority and the conversation dropped.

WITH A COUPLE of hours still to go before the fundraiser began, Jack entered the hall dressed in his rented tuxedo. He had gotten a topaz bow tie to match Melanie's dress since they were cohosting the event. Scanning the large room, he didn't see her there yet. She'd told him she had planned to decorate with Shelby earlier in the day, and by the looks of it they had done an amazing job. Several tall Christmas trees lined the walls of the ballroom and had unwrapped toys surrounding their trunks. Garlands and ornaments in red, gold and silver hung from the boughs, interspersed with smaller toys. It looked like a child's fantasy Christmas land. The only things missing were Santa and the elves.

"Mr. Cuthbert, the catering manager was looking for you or Ms. Beach. Do you have a moment to speak with her?"

Jack turned toward the server who wore a white shirt and black pants, blending in with the other staff who were dressed identically. "I'll be right there."

He passed a table and straightened the tablecloth as another server approached him. "The deejay asked where you wanted her to set up. And the florist dropped off the corsages you requested."

Last-minute details requiring his attention took up his time as Jack delegated, managed and directed the staff. This was his first, and hopefully his last, attempt at running the annual family fundraiser. The donated toys and money would go toward making sure that every child in their community got a Christmas gift, a worthwhile effort, but this running the show bit was not for him. His talents rested in donating money, not raising it. He'd gladly hand the reins back to Shelby next year.

Speaking of his cousin, she strode toward him from the opposite side of the hall. "You clean up pretty good, cuz."

"Back at you."

She wore a silvery-blue dress that matched her Cuthbert-blue eyes. She held a hand to her belly. "I don't remember being this nervous last year, but my stomach is in knots. Have you seen Melanie yet?"

"No, sorry. I've been solving last-minute crises for the last hour."

"I'm sure she said that she'd be here by now."

As if cued, the double doors to the lobby opened and framed Melanie in her topaz gown that was complemented by the gold-and-pearl necklace she wore around her long elegant neck. Jack's breath caught in his throat, and he coughed to disguise it.

Shelby nudged him before she strode to-ward Melanie. "Jack was just asking about you."

She turned to him. "Is everything okay?"

His tongue felt as if it had swollen to three times its size so that he could only nod and grunt an agreement. She looked fantastic. No, more than fantastic. She looked like a fantasy brought to life just for him.

He shook his head. Not for him. She was with Marius. He cleared his throat and tried to speak. "You're beautiful."

"Don't act so surprised." But she gave a slight curtsy. "But thank you for the com-pliment, sir." She glanced around the room. "Everything looks ready." She turned her golden-brown eyes on him. "Are you okay? You look a little flushed."

Shelby bumped his arm. "He's nervous about speaking in public in front of so many people. He does better with a room full of dogs and cats."

"I think it's the dancing that's making me more nervous." He pulled at the collar of his shirt where his neck seemed to have swelled. "It is a little warm in here, don't you think? Maybe I should have them turn down the thermostat a few degrees before we fill the room with a bunch of people."

"The temperature's fine, Jack. It's you that's overheated."

He gave Shelby a quick glare, then held out his elbow to Mel. "The deejay wanted to go ask us questions about the order of the program. Shall we?"

She clasped his arm and walked with him to the deejay stand where the woman listened to music on headphones, but took them off as they approached. "I've got the list of music here, but I wanted to make sure when you wanted each played during the evening."

By the time they finished confirming

the musical selections, guests had started to enter the hall. Jack reached for Mel's hand. "Before you go, I got you a little something for tonight."

He held her hand as they walked behind the makeshift stage at the end of the hall where he'd left her corsage. She gasped when he pulled out the orchid with the gold ribbon from its box. "I've always loved orchids."

He'd known that when he'd ordered this weeks ago. He pulled the straight pin from the base of the corsage. "I figured that you deserved to have something special after all your hard work for the fundraiser."

"I'm not the only one who worked on this though, and I didn't get you anything."

He held up the flower. "Would you prefer to pin it on yourself or may I do the honors?"

"You may."

He put a finger under one of the golden straps on her dress and grazed her warm skin underneath before placing the corsage onto the dress and pinning it in place. The flower drooped to one side, so he had to adjust it and pin it more securely to her dress. He stepped back, surveying it. "Looks straight."

She tilted her head down and inhaled the fragrance from the orchid. "It's beautiful. Thank you, Jack."

He looked into her eyes and felt his chest tighten as he thought about her. He should tell her that his feelings for her had changed.

He should keep his mouth shut.

No, she'd had the courage to tell him before, and he should find the guts to tell her that he loved her too. That he wanted her and her alone.

But before he could decide what to say to her, she glanced over his shoulder and gasped. "Dad?"

WHAT WAS HER dad doing here? Had he mentioned that he was coming to the fundraiser during their last phone call? As Mel remembered it, they had only discussed the upcoming holidays and his plans with her stepmother to travel through New Mexico. Nothing about returning to Michigan before Christmas. She hurried as fast as she could to him on high heels and gave him a hug. He patted one of her bare shoulders. He'd never been one to show her affection around others. Or ever at all, if she was being honest. Still, it was good to see him. "Why didn't you say you were going to be in town?"

"It was a last-minute decision." He looked past her and gave a nod to Jack who had followed her. "Your friend thought it might be nice if we came to see you for this."

Jack had invited him? She turned and smiled at him, overcome with emotions. "You asked my dad to come up and see me?"

He shrugged as if it was no big deal, but it was to her. She threw her arms around him and hugged him. He gave her waist a squeeze and pulled her closer to him. She closed her eyes and tried to quell the tears that threatened to ruin her mascara. She didn't know what to say without sounding sappy and overly sentimental. "Thank you," she finally whispered in his ear. Simple words that held more meaning than she could manage at the moment.

"You're welcome." He planted a quick

kiss on her cheek, and she let him go. "I've saved seats for your family at our table." He pointed behind himself. "I'll let you guys catch up while I take care of some final things."

He left, and she turned back to her dad. "I can't believe you're here. Thank you for coming up here, Dad. This means so much to me."

"I couldn't exactly refuse when Jack sent us the airline tickets, could I?" He looked her over. "You're different somehow. New haircut?"

"I figured it was time for a change. You like it?" When he didn't answer, she glanced behind him. "Where's Betty? Didn't she come here with you?"

"She had to make a stop in the ladies' room first." He pointed around the hall and nodded. "This looks good in here."

"It was a lot of hard work, but hopefully our efforts will pay off tonight with more donations."

"Don, did you see the Fletchers are here? I haven't seen them in forever." Her stepmother joined them and looked Melanie over. Their relationship had never been close since her dad had married Betty a few years ago. "Melanie."

She gave her a nod. "Betty."

Betty tugged on her dad's arm. "I told the Fletchers we would sit with them."

"But Jack saved you both seats with me at the family table."

"Oh." Betty's face soured. "It's just that we haven't seen the Fletchers since we moved to Florida. And I promised them we would spend the evening with them." She gave her dad a huge smile. "Don, they're thinking of moving south for the winter, and I was telling them about that condo in the next section over from ours that went up for sale last week. They'd like to get your opinion on it."

Mel's dad looked at her, then over to the other side of the room where an older couple stood, watching them and waving. "Lionel and I go way back. You don't mind, do you? We'll catch up later."

Mel didn't have a chance to protest before they walked away from her. She would be pretty busy during the evening, and there was Marius to consider too. Better they should sit with their friends. Her dad was right. They could catch up later.

She turned and walked to the family table, trying not to let their rejection sting.

By the time the hall had filled, the conversation and noise level had risen so that Mel had to lean in close to Aunt Sarah to hear what she was saying. "I asked where your young man was."

Mel searched the guests but didn't see Marius among them. "He said he might be running a little late, depending on his patient load today."

"He's a doctor?"

"No, he's a nurse in the emergency room."

Aunt Sarah nodded and motioned to Henry who leaned forward in his wheelchair. "What was the name of that young nurse you had last time at the hospital? The one who joked about old veins?"

Henry Duffy shut his eyes, squeezing them tight as if trying to conjure up the name. "It's on the tip of my tongue. Started with an *N*, maybe?"

"Marius, you made it on time," Mel said as he joined her and kissed her cheek.

Henry frowned. "Nope. That's not it." He opened his eyes and looked at Marius. "It's this guy."

"His name is Marius, and he's my date tonight."

Henry glanced at Aunt Sarah. "I thought you said she was in love with Jack."

Aunt Sarah shushed him as Mel linked her arm with Marius. "No, I'm with Marius. I'm just emceeing and dancing with Jack tonight. Speaking of…" She spied the stage and took in the crowded room. "It's almost time to kick off the evening."

She started to take a step away from Marius, but he reached out for her hand. "Can it wait just a second while I tell you how amazing you look?"

His compliment took some of the sting out of her father's rebuff. She glanced down at her dress, then at the orchid. "Thank you for the compliment. But I need to find Jack."

She found him talking to the deejay who gave him a microphone. He turned at her approach. "Ready to get this started?" He looked over at the family table. "Where's your dad? I thought they were sitting with us."

"Betty found friends of theirs that they haven't seen in a while, so they changed seats to their table instead."

Jack peered into her face. "Are you okay with that?"

"Does it really matter?" She gripped the microphone tighter. "Let's just get this started."

"I didn't bring them here for them to ignore you. Should I ask them to move back to our table?" He waited for her answer. "Mel, they should be sitting with you."

She didn't want him to make a big deal out of this because there was no point. Her dad would do what he preferred whether she wanted him to or not. "Drop it, okay?"

"But you were so excited to see your dad. You should have seen the look on your face when you realized that he was here. I don't like to see him hurt you again. You deserve better."

"I do, but it's complicated, and now's not the time. We have a fundraiser to start." She pointed to the microphone. "Let's make this the best event this town has ever seen.

Something they'll be talking about for years to come."

Jack returned her smile, and they walked to the stage together.

DINNER HAD BEEN served and cleared, and Jack felt as if he was going to get sick all over his rented tux. The dancing competition was about to begin, and he didn't think that he could go through with it. But he wasn't going to disappoint Mel again this evening.

He glanced across the hall to where he saw her parents talking with another couple and laughing. Her dad couldn't have given Mel one night of his attention? It seemed to him that ever since Mel's mom had died, her dad had ignored his daughter. Maybe it was because he didn't know what to do with a girl. Or because Mel resembled her mother so much. Whatever the reason, it didn't excuse the neglect. Mel deserved better than that from the only family she had left.

The woman in question tapped her wrist where her watch would normally have rested. Instead, she wore a thin silver bracelet there. "We should get the dancing started."

Shelby kicked him under the table. "People are going to leave if you don't keep the program going. And we'll lose out on the money they would have pledged if they had stayed."

He stood and held out his hand to Mel. "We're the first couple. Shall we?"

The deejay dimmed the lights and music as Mel accepted the microphone. "Ladies and gentlemen, thank you again for coming this evening. As a special treat during dessert, several couples have prepared dances for your enjoyment. Please vote for your favorite couple by donating money to the bucket with their names located by the chocolate fountain. To start things off, Jack Cuthbert and I will perform a rumba."

The guests clapped lightly as they took their positions on the dance floor, a spotlight on their figures. Jack took a deep breath as he held out his hand to Mel who clasped it and placed her other hand on his right shoulder just as they had learned from Monsieur LeBlanc. They stood, looking into each other's eyes as their music started to play. Hoping he'd remember the steps, he moved his left foot forward and stepped to the side with his right, swaying his hips in the figure eight pattern and hoping he didn't appear too stiff.

"Look at me," Mel said, keeping her gaze on him. "Stop thinking of everyone out there and concentrate on me."

He followed her directions and led her into the first underarm turn. Remembering Monsieur's instructions to move his hand over her as if giving Mel a halo, he turned her, then brought her close again. He smiled at her. "One down."

"Three more to go."

The music seemed to thrum inside of him as he moved Mel through the steps of the dance. Pushing her away only to draw her back into his embrace. The give. And the take. They danced to one side of the floor, then swayed as they moved to the other. A pause had him dip Mel, then pull her slowly up to stare into her face.

"You're doing great," she whispered before they did another underarm turn followed quickly by another in the opposite direction.

"We're almost there."

All these practices with Mel seemed to be paying off as they moved into the last section of the song. But the hardest portion was coming up. Mel would drag her foot on the floor as he turned them in a circle before pulling her into a tight embrace and letting her go once more. Monsieur Le-Blanc had told him it was like letting the one you loved go.

But Jack didn't want to let Mel go. Yes, she was with Marius. But if he hadn't messed up when she'd confessed her feelings, they would likely be together right now.

Mel put out her foot, and Jack turned them in the circle. Then he pulled her to him, and she clasped his shoulders.

Don't let her go. Hold her tight just a moment more.

But he released her, and she danced away, him trailing behind her.

The finale was coming up, and he hoped that he'd get it right this time. He grasped her waist and pulled her back, swaying to the right, together, left, together. Then he turned her in his arms so that she faced him, their faces close. Then dipped her back before pulling her up. Staring into each other's eyes as they swayed once more. And then, a connection, a bond was made. Something deep, that went beyond their friendship. Could he name it? He wanted to, but he was still unsure of himself, of what he could offer Mel. He did the last underarm turn and brought her into a tight hold, their chests heaving from the exertion but also the tension that seemed to have spilled out in front of their audience. She smiled and glanced down as they completed the final move of Mel sliding to the floor and held it.

Then applause broke the spell that Jack had found himself under. He helped Mel to her feet and they gave a small bow, holding hands. He kept her hand in his as they moved to the side and the deejay announced the next couple.

MEL NEEDED SOME AIR. She spotted a nearby side exit and stepped outside, embracing the chilly temperature.

Successfully executing the dance had set her pulse to racing, not to mention being that close to Jack. It had been exhilarating, and she tried to push down those feelings. This time it was Jack who joined her. "That was awesome." She smiled at him, unable to hold her joy in any longer.

"I couldn't have never done that without you, Mel. You're one of a kind."

"Ha. So are you."

"You're special. So kind. And funny. You're—" And the next thing she knew, Jack was kissing her. And kissing her as if he meant it. Mel closed her eyes and allowed the sweet sensation to continue.

Then reason reentered her brain, and she pushed against his chest and he released her.

"Sorry, Mel. That was wrong."

His apology lessened the impact of the kiss. She put her hand to her lips that still tingled. "Why did you do that?"

"I don't know." She put a hand on his shoulder, and he looked at her. "You're with Marius."

"Yes, I am."

"But I have to know something." He took her hand and squeezed. "Do you love him?"

"What?"

"Are you in love with him?"

His eyes seemed to seek hers, but she couldn't keep his gaze. Had to shut her eyes so that he couldn't see the turmoil his questions sent her. "Why are you asking me this?"

"Not so long ago, you told me you loved me. That you wanted a future with me." She nodded, unsure what else to do. "Please, Mel, look at me." She opened her eyes and stared into his. "Do you still feel the same way?"

She let go of his hand and stepped away. "What do you think you're doing?"

"I'm asking if you still love me."

"I've been trying to get over you for the last seven weeks, and you ask me if I still love you?" For a second, she wondered if this was a dream, or maybe a nightmare? "You have no right to ask me these questions now."

"I think I'm in love with you, Mel."

"You *think* you are?" She frowned at him. "You mean, you don't know if you are or not?"

He put a hand on his head. "These past

couple of weeks have been confusing, and I'm not sure what I'm feeling."

"Well, that's not good enough." The turmoil that had threatened to drown her now turned into a hot streak of anger. "The only reason that you *think* you're in love with me is because I have a real chance with someone else. And you can't stand the idea that I might not be in your life at every moment."

"That's not it."

"When do you *think* you started feeling this way? When someone started to show me attention and take up my free time?"

Jack didn't answer, but his sheepish grimace was answer enough. She closed her eyes. Seven weeks ago, she would have loved to be hearing these words, but not like this. "I am not a toy that you can pout over when someone else starts to play with me. I have a chance at a real relationship, and I am not going to let you spoil that for me."

"Do you love him, Mel?"

"No." She didn't love Marius. "Not yet. But I want this chance to see if I could."

The side door opened, and one of the

chefs walked out with a bag of trash. Mel used the opportunity to slip back inside alone.

JACK RETURNED TO the hall to find the last couple, Shelby and Josh, completing their dance. Mel appeared at the deejay's table with the microphone. "Don't forget to vote for your favorite couple by donating to their bucket stationed by the dessert table. We'll announce the winners after you all get a chance to try your own dance moves on the floor."

The deejay went right into a song with a fast tempo. Several couples walked to the dance floor, but Jack wasn't interested in them. Only one person in this entire hall was important to him, and she had made it clear that she didn't want to be with him.

Why had he kissed Mel? He'd told himself it was a bad idea even as he'd pressed his lips to hers and found a willing partner.

Only to be pushed away.

Was this how she had felt on Halloween when he'd turned her away? Was this heart-crushing, soul-devastating loss what she had gone through?

He felt a hand on his shoulder and turned to find Aunt Sarah standing there. "You and Melanie did a wonderful job this year on the fundraiser. You should be proud of yourselves."

He gave a nod, not trusting his voice. Aunt Sarah gestured at Mel dancing with her date. "She's not in love with him."

Jack turned to look at her. "Not yet. But she will be."

"If you don't do something first, then yes. You'll have lost her for good." She tapped her lips with a finger. "But I don't think that's what you want. You love her."

"I always have."

"But you're too afraid to go after her."

He nodded slowly, then watched as Mel laughed at something Marius said. "If I loved and lost her... That's the one thing I couldn't bear. It's better that we stay friends."

"Better for whom?"

He shook his head, disappointed with himself more than anything. "I've got to get back to work. This fundraiser doesn't run itself, you know."

"You always immerse yourself in work

when you're running scared. Someday, you'll discover that staying busy doesn't keep you company. That it's the relationships you have that make life have meaning." She put a hand on his arm. "That's what my sister told you before she died."

Aunt Sarah was mistaken. "No, she made me promise to not give up on holding on to love."

"So why have you?"

He looked into his great-aunt's eyes that were so much like Nana's. He missed his grandmother at the holidays. She'd had a way of making them special that no one else had. Not even Shelby with all her fantastic planning could make the holidays the way they used to be. "I see the catering manager trying to get my attention. I've got to go."

He hurried away before he did something like cry over what would never be.

MEL DOUBLE COUNTED the money in Shelby and Josh's jar to make sure she had the right total. If anything, she appreciated this distraction after the disastrous kiss with Jack earlier.

How dare he kiss her now! Why would he suddenly change his mind about them if not only because he knew that she could fall for Marius? And his declaration only confused her more.

What if she did pursue Jack like she'd always wanted? But then what if he changed his mind back to saying they were only friends? She'd be left alone. Again.

She faltered as she laid the twenty-dollar bills on the table. She'd lost count again. Twenty, forty, sixty…

She paused her counting to look across the table at Jack who made notations on the pad beside him. After they'd returned to the ballroom post-kiss, he seemed to be making an effort to ignore her. Just as well. She was here with Marius. And it wasn't fair to her date to be thinking about someone else.

Even if she couldn't get Jack out of her mind. Why did he have to kiss her tonight of all nights?

She groaned which brought Jack's head up, his eyes meeting hers. "What's wrong?"

"Nothing."

He gave a quick nod of his head and returned to counting money. Beside her, Shelby wrote down her totals of the votes and slid the paper to Mel. "My counts agree with yours." She turned to Jack. "Have you finished?"

He shook his head, keeping his gaze down at the notepad.

"Why are you so grumpy? I thought you'd be relieved after finishing the dance. Besides, tonight has been a huge success. This dance competition idea of Aunt Sarah's raised more than twice as much money as we did last year." Shelby turned to Mel and asked, "Do you know what's wrong with him?"

"It's nothing." She finished counting and wrote the number down. "My totals agree with yours. But since the results are so close, should we count it again?"

"Counting again won't change it." Jack passed the notepad across the table and stood. "Just announce the winner so we can finish this up and go home."

He moved away from the table. Shelby rolled her eyes. "He can be so melodramatic sometimes. Just because you guys didn't win…"

Mel didn't disabuse her of that notion. Better to let her think that Jack's competitive side hurt over their fourth-place showing in the competition rather than what had happened earlier. "Guess I should let everyone know who won then."

"You two should be proud of tonight's event. You both make a great team."

"Don't, Shel."

"What? I was merely observing that you work well together. Nothing else."

Mel gave her a sidelong look but let the comment pass. Because the truth was that they did make a great team. Whether it was running a fundraiser or dancing, they made it work even under circumstances that didn't.

The deejay changed to a slow song that had been popular when she was in high school, and Mel closed her eyes. She'd always carried this fantasy of dancing cheek-to-cheek with Jack to it one day. "We can announce the winner after this song."

"It was always one of your favorites."

Shelby looked around the ballroom. "Where's Josh? I feel the need to dance."

Mel watched her friend leave in pursuit of her husband. Songs like this always made her arms feel emptier.

A tap on her shoulder, and she turned to find Marius standing there with his hand outstretched. "Care to dance?"

She nodded. Her arms didn't have to be empty. Not anymore.

On the dance floor, Marius placed his clasped hands at the base of her spine as she rested her head on his shoulder and swayed to the romantic ballad. "What's wrong?" he asked her after a while.

She shook her head, not wanting to voice the melancholy that had settled on her shoulders like a thin gossamer shawl. She could swipe it away, but she let it cover her for now. "It's nothing."

"Your mood changed after you danced with Jack."

Mel let her eyes roam until they found the man across the hall watching her dance now with Marius. He turned away and left the room. She sighed. "Maybe I'm just tired."

"Is that all this is?"

She nodded and placed her cheek to Marius's solid form. "Just hold me and dance."

"With pleasure."

AFTER HIS SISTER and her husband claimed the trophy for the couples' dance, Jack knew the evening had ended. At least for him. Sure, the deejay would play a few more songs for those who wanted to make the evening last a little longer, but in his mind it was over when Mel had rejected him.

Mel's father approached him and shook his hand. "Thank you again for the plane tickets to come back to Michigan. The wife and I had a wonderful time."

"Did your daughter?"

Mr. Beach frowned at his words. "Melanie? I don't know if she did."

"You wouldn't know because you didn't spend even a minute with her." Jack shook his head. "Do you know anything about her life now?"

"We talk."

"Over the phone. Twice a month. I

know." He looked at the man who had fathered such a wonderful woman and wondered how Mel had turned out the way she had. "She's your only child, and you don't deserve her."

He started to walk away, but Mr. Beach followed him. "You don't know what it's like to lose your wife and have to raise a little girl on your own."

Jack turned back. "You're right. But I do know that Mel felt abandoned. Holidays. Birthdays. Every day. She did nothing but love you, and you've done nothing to warrant such devotion. Even now, she's probably justifying the fact that you spent your entire evening talking to someone else instead of her. And how it's okay that you didn't spend time with her because the two of you will have another chance to catch up. But what if you don't? When your wife died, you lost your daughter too. Surely, it should have brought you two closer. She's become more my family than yours."

"So why did you send us the tickets?"

"Because I hoped that you would finally see that your relationship with Mel was important. That it was worth fighting for."

"I don't need a lecture from you. You have no clue what you're talking about."

Mr. Beach turned on his heel and returned to his wife. Jack watched as the two of them left without a word to Mel, who also observed their hasty departure.

Well, that hadn't gone as he'd planned.

He realized he wanted to fight for Mel now. But admitted it was too late.

CHAPTER ELEVEN

MEL RUBBED THE sleep from her eyes and stared across the table at the empty seat her father had vacated minutes before. He'd called her that Sunday morning, asking if they could meet before he and Betty left for Florida again. She took it as a hopeful sign.

She stirred more sugar into her coffee and waited for her father to return to their table. After all, this was his invitation. And it was also the first time she'd heard from him since the night of the fundraiser two days before.

She could pretend that his snub that night hadn't hurt, but what would that prove? That she would accept his continued indifference? But no more.

Finally, her father returned to their table with two cinnamon rolls that he'd bought from the bakery counter. He handed her one of the plates. The spicy smell of the cinnamon enticed her, but she swallowed her disappointment and turned her gaze out the window.

"So what are your plans for Christmas?"

She turned back to look at him as he popped a piece of the sweet roll into his mouth. "The usual. Cuthbert family party on Christmas Eve. Then spending the next day reading at home alone."

He frowned. "You spend Christmas Day alone? I thought you got together with those friends of yours."

"No, that's what you and Betty do, Dad. I'm on the couch with a good book. And you know what? I enjoy it. I don't mind being by myself."

"I always minded it. After your mother died—" He gave a cough and dropped his gaze to the napkin sitting underneath his coffee cup, adjusting it with his fingers. "I couldn't stand my own company. The silence. The absence. The empty space on the other side of the bed."

"But now you have Betty to keep you company."

Her dad looked back up at her, a pain in his eyes that she remembered from after her mom had died. He gave a half-shrug. "She's company, you're right, but I still love your mother. For me, it's always been her."

"But Mom's gone and has been for years. You have to move on."

"She may not be physically here, but she's never been completely gone from my heart." He gave her a sad smile. "I'll never love anyone like I love her. Don't get me wrong. Betty's fun, and I like her a lot. But she will never be your mother. Could never replace her."

Mel gave a nod. She could understand his love for her mother since she missed her dearly too. "Can I ask why you avoid me?"

"I don't avoid you."

Mel shot him a look. She didn't believe that for a second since she rarely saw him. "What do you call using every excuse to not come back to Michigan to see me? Or invite me down to Florida?"

"Because I miss your mother more when you're around. You remind me so much of her. Your eyes. Your smile. It's all her." He tore a piece off his cinnamon roll, but didn't eat it. "Even your books are her." He glanced up at her. "She'd love that little shop of yours."

Mel had designed it with her mother in mind, especially the children's section with different characters populating the space. When her mother read her bedtime stories, she'd spun the tale so that Mel could see the people of the story. Her mother should have been a writer since she'd been a gifted storyteller. Books had been her treasure, and she'd passed that love to Mel.

Mel reached out and touched her father's hand. "Dad, since Mom died I feel as if I've lost you too. You're alive and well, but you're so distant that I feel that loss too."

He stiffened and removed his hand from her touch. "You don't know what you're asking from me."

"I do know. I want to spend time with you. You're the only family I've got."

He stuffed the rest of his sweet roll into his mouth, then washed the bite down with the remains of his coffee. He stood abruptly. "I should get going. I have to pick up Betty from the hotel, then we're off to the airport."

Mel stood as he started to put on his coat. "Dad, don't push me away. I feel as if you've finally opened up a little to me. Don't run off now when we've got the chance to make this right."

Her father sat down again and rubbed the back of his neck. "It's hard for me to talk about this stuff. Feelings and all."

"I get it, but I need you to talk to me about this." She sat back down too and reached to put her hand over his. "I don't want to look back years from now and wonder what we might have had if we had tried harder to be a family. I want more than talking to you on the phone a couple of times a month, don't you?"

Her dad nodded, and it gave her a glimmer of hope. "Good. Let's see each other more. I'm taking time off after the holidays to unwind. I could come down and visit you in Florida."

He gave a soft smile. "I'd like that."

Mel raised one eyebrow. "You would?"

"Of course I would." He took her fingers in his and squeezed. "I'd like nothing better than to see you. And I promise to try harder. I don't want to have any more regrets with you."

He glanced at his watch. "I wish I could stay longer and chat, but I really do have to go." He stood and wrapped the scarf around his neck, then gave her a long look. "Maybe it's not my place to say this, but you should really consider dating that Jack Cuthbert."

"We're just friends."

"How many 'just friends' would send plane tickets to your parents for a visit? Think about it." He leaned forward and gave her a quick peck on the cheek. "I love you, Melanie. Please don't ever forget that. You'll always be my daughter, no matter what."

"No matter what."

He rubbed his thumb over her hand. "That's right. I'll call you when we get home."

"Love you too, Dad."

HE WAS ONLY a few minutes late, but Jack could see the anger radiating off Stacey when he walked in the door of the restaurant. He hustled over to her. "Thanks for the invite, Stacey. Sorry about the delay. I had a last-minute patient that took longer than I expected."

He was surprised when Stacey had called and suggested they have dinner. But in the moment, it had seemed like an olive branch, and he was in no position to turn one of those down.

Given Stacey's mood, which he should have anticipated, maybe this was a mistake.

She didn't say a word to him but gave a nod to the hostess who then came forward with a couple of menus in her arms. She led them through a maze of tables and seated them at one near a window, leaving the menus with them. Stacey grabbed one and opened it with a snap. Jack reached over and lowered the menu to catch her gaze. "Stace, I told you I was sorry."

"But are you really, Jack?" She pushed the menu higher to block her view of him. "How many times did you call and tell me you were running late? That you had one more patient to see?"

Glimpses of the past nudged his brain, but he pushed those memories aside. This was a chance to find out if they could do things differently. To possibly make it work if that's what they wanted. "By now, you should understand how committed I am to my patients."

"By now, I'd assumed you'd changed."

"Caring for my animals will never change." He pursed his lips as he gazed at his ex-wife. "I thought we were going to be up front and honest with each other this time around."

Stacey dropped the menu to the table. "You want me to be honest? Fine. I can be honest." She lowered her voice as if suddenly aware that people were watching them. "But you need to tell me the truth first. Do you really want us to get back together?"

He had been about to reassure her since that's what he'd been thinking about, but the words wouldn't come out of his mouth. Instead, he stared back at her. He needed to be as honest with her as he wanted her to be with him. "No, I don't."

Her mouth opened, then closed into a tight line as she glared at him. "This is about Melanie, isn't it? I heard about the dance you two did at the fundraiser. In fact, I saw it. You remember my friend Deedee? She was there with her husband and recorded the whole thing. Couldn't wait to show me how the two of you danced together."

"It was merely a dance." Just as it had been merely a kiss between them after. Mel had made it clear that there wasn't anything between them. "It didn't mean anything."

"I saw the way you two looked at each other." Stacey shook her head as if disappointed in him. "Just admit it. You're in love with her."

Again, he opened his mouth to protest but he couldn't. Images of Mel laughing, Mel challenging him, Mel showing him how much she cared about him all ran together.

Stacey's frown deepened. "I'm doing my best to give us another chance, but you're still trying to figure out how you feel about Melanie."

"My feelings for Mel are complicated."

"I still love you, Jack. Can you honestly tell me that you love me too?"

"I loved you once."

"Once…"

He reached out and took her hand in his. "I'll always love her, that's the truth."

She snatched her hand back as if he'd burned it. "I was fooling myself thinking that this time could be different with us. After seeing you again, I thought that we could make things work out. I'd planned on moving back in with you after a couple of weeks if everything went well."

This time, he was the one to narrow his eyes at her. "Wasn't I going to get a say in this decision of yours?" Shades of their past when Stacey had mapped out their lives with little of his input made his stomach clench.

She gave a chuckle and tossed her head. "You would have gone along with it if I had told you what I was planning."

"Why? Because I always jumped when you said to before?" He'd asked the question, but he already knew the answer to that one. Their server arrived at the table which stopped the conversation for a moment. Stacey ordered her usual white wine spritzer, then the server turned to him. He thought of Mel who had started to order different things to find something new that she might like.

Well, he wasn't Mel. He liked things to stay as they were. Things to stay in a comfortable zone where he didn't need to question the status quo.

But sitting across from his ex-wife now, he realized that maybe Mel had the right idea. When things didn't work, you had to try something new even if it was uncomfortable. Stacey had liked being able to control him, and he'd let her for a while in their marriage since it was easier than always disagreeing. However, this time around, he wasn't about to let her think he could be so easily manipulated. Jack turned back to Stacey. "I think I need to leave."

The server's eyes widened, and she turned on her heel and left the table while Stacey continued to frown at him. "Why? It's just dinner, and we're talking about our future."

"But you want more than what I can give you."

"Let me guess. You're going to run to

Melanie and tell her all about how you turned me down. How you got some kind of closure after all this time."

He got to his feet, and she rose beside him, placing a hand on his arm. "We're both hungry and angry and taking it out on each other. Let's sit down and discuss this over dinner like grown adults."

"I don't think there's anything left to discuss." He started to smile. "I always wondered what would happen if I saw you again. If we tried to make things work. And now I know. So thank you, Stacey, for giving me closure on this. It feels pretty good to be the one leaving you this time."

He grabbed his coat and exited the restaurant, feeling better than he had in a while. Shelby had been right, too, about looking up previous relationships to find out what had gone wrong. Who knew that closing the door on all the what-ifs would feel so liberating?

He practically danced his way out to his car.

AFTER ANOTHER BUSY day of Christmas shoppers at the bookstore, Mel wished to go home, take a long bubble bath and then spend the rest of her evening reading in bed. But she'd made plans with Marius. And as much as she might want to postpone them, she knew that she needed to keep her commitment to him.

He had been given tickets for a Detroit symphony concert to hear the orchestra perform favorite Christmas songs, and they planned to catch a late dinner afterward. Because it was a dressy event, she had chosen to wear the burgundy velvet dress that Kristina had assured her would get her through all the holiday gatherings. So here Mel was. She adjusted the straps of her heels, then straightened to look up at Marius as he approached her from the bar, two drinks in his hands. It was intermission during the concert, and she should be enjoying herself. Instead she couldn't stop thinking about Jack.

It had been over a week since the fundraiser, and she hadn't heard a single word from Jack. Not a text. Not a call. Nothing.

She should be beyond letting his silence hurt her, but it wounded her more than she was prepared to admit. Her heart had calluses from past wounds, but only Jack could injure her this deep.

She glanced over at Marius who put a hand around her waist and pulled her closer to his side. He was a good man. One she could possibly love someday.

Or maybe she could if Jack didn't already hold that place in her heart. What would it take to remove him? Would he always be the one she wanted to be with? Why couldn't she move on and give Marius a real chance? But the truth was that she couldn't. And it wasn't fair to Marius to keep stringing him along like this.

He must have sensed her watching him because he turned to her and gave her a smile. If only it could make her forget Jack.

"We need to talk."

The words were out of her mouth before she could stop them. Marius frowned and took his arm away from her. "About what?"

"Us."

He sighed. Did he know this was coming? As of earlier this evening, she had planned to keep seeing him. Hoped that her feelings would change if she gave it more time. That she could fall in love with this man standing beside her. The only thing she'd wanted more than that was for the man she loved to love her back. But wishing hadn't made it happen.

"Couldn't we talk about this after the concert?"

Maybe he was right. They could enjoy the concert, then discuss this over dinner. But even as she thought that, she knew she couldn't put this off for a moment more. "If I don't say this now, I might lose my courage."

He placed his wineglass on the table. "I know what you're going to say."

"You do?"

"I've felt that things have been different since the night of the fundraiser." He searched her eyes, and she wondered if he could see the reluctance she felt so acutely. "It's Jack, isn't it?"

She gave a soft nod, unable to deny the words. "It's always been him." She put a hand on his arm, but he drew it away from her touch. "I really wanted to love you. And I tried. You want us to get serious about each other, but it's not right for me to do this to you while I hope these feelings for him go away."

"Does he know?"

She shook her head.

"Are you going to tell him?"

Again, she shook her head. She'd been down that road before and knew how it ended. No thank you.

Marius took a deep breath and adjusted the lapels of his suit jacket. "The intermission is almost over. Do you want to stay for the rest of the concert?"

"Only if you want to."

He paused and glanced around the crowded bar area. "I'm not in a festive mood anymore. Let's just go."

The drive back to her house was heavy with a silence that neither of them could break. When they reached her front door at home, Marius didn't say a word as she unlocked it and turned to look at him. "I understand you're disappointed, Marius. Again, I'm sorry about all this. I hope you find someone special, who loves you the way that you deserve."

Marius began to walk away, but stopped

and faced her. "I am hurt, Melanie, but I wish you find the same."

She called Shelby as soon as she entered her house and collapsed on her bed. She'd left it unmade that morning since she'd been in a hurry to get to work and unpack the delivery of new books before the store opened. Her friend answered on the first ring. "I was about to call you with my news. Are you sitting down?"

She was actually draped across the end of her bed staring at the ceiling. "Ha. You're pregnant."

Shelby gasped on the other end. "How did you know?"

"You've been refusing alcohol for the last few weeks, and you turned up your nose at the shrimp appetizers at the fundraiser. The same ones you devoured at last year's party."

Shelby giggled on the other end. "Can you believe it? In the space of a year, I'll have become a wife and mother." Another pause followed by a groan. "Wait a minute. What have I done? This is not like me at all. I plan for these things. I don't let them happen by accident."

"This is no more an accident than you falling in love with Josh. Sure, you didn't have it written in ink on your calendar, but you want this and you made it happen."

"You're right. I do want this life. I'm so happy and grateful I've found it and more." Shelby asked, "I thought you were going out with Marius tonight? Wait. What happened?"

Mel closed her eyes and sighed. "We broke up." Best to rip off that bandage and feel the momentary sting.

"Why? I thought you liked him."

"I did. I do." She took a deep breath. "But it would never have worked out between us."

"Because of Jack."

"Yes. Because I could never give Marius my whole heart when Jack will always hold a part of it."

"Oh, Mel." Shelby sounded disappointed in her. "I thought you had moved on from him."

"How do I move on from the love of my life? Everyone makes it sound like it's so easy. I can't just turn off these feelings I've had for most of my life. Just forget the way he made me feel." She sat up and grabbed a pillow to hug to her chest. Dickens looked up at her from his side of the bed. "And the thing is Jack told me that he loved me too. But I rejected him."

"He did what? When?"

"The night of the fundraiser. Right after we danced. Told me that he loved me and wanted me. But he was only saying that because Marius was in the picture."

"How do you know that?"

"Because he told me that he's confused about this. He wanted to know if I still loved him, but he wasn't sure about his feelings." Mel groaned and shook her head. "I'm so foolish, aren't I? I let go of a sure thing only to end up alone once again."

"You never said a word about this. We talk every day, but you never mentioned anything. How come?"

Because she hadn't wanted to acknowledge that Jack's admission had made her question what she should do. That his kiss hadn't left her thoughts since that night. And that because of that her breakup with Marius had been inevitable. "It doesn't matter anyway." Silence fell between them until Mel straightened and tossed the pillow aside. "You know what? Let's focus instead on your good news. I can't believe you're going to have a baby." She smiled. "That's so great. Especially to find out around Christmas."

"We've decided to tell our parents on Christmas Day, but we're holding off on telling the entire family until I'm further along." Shelby paused. "You are going to be there at the Cuthbert annual Christmas Eve party, aren't you?"

It was tradition for Mel to close the bookstore early on Christmas Eve, then attend the Cuthberts' huge party where they invited the whole family and included as many friends and neighbors as would fit in the house. It was the one thing at Christmas that Mel looked forward to the most. She'd planned on asking Marius to go with her this year, but that was out of the question now. "I wouldn't miss it. It's my favorite event at Christmas." An image of Jack popped into her head. "Will Jack be there?"

"According to Penny, he's promised to

take the night off from the clinic. What are you thinking?"

She thought about what it would mean to see him again, knowing she wasn't going to be with Marius and also knowing that Jack had feelings for her. She cast aside the image of Jack smiling at her. She didn't need romance at this point. It would be better to put all thoughts of that away until she could be stronger.

After all, she was going to be an aunt— soft of—she should focus on that. She let out a laugh, and warned, "Prepare for your baby to get really spoiled. This is the closest I'll get to being an aunt, and I plan on buying the biggest presents. And plenty of books. This kid is going to be a reader the minute she's born."

"She, huh? I think it's too early to tell."

"Oh, it's a she. I can feel it."

"I'm sorry about Marius. And about Jack."

"Don't be. I'm perfectly fine being on my own."

CHRISTMAS EVE'S ANNUAL Cuthbert family party didn't look the same this year as it had in the past. Jack sipped his cup of eggnog and let his gaze linger over members of his family, both immediate and extended. During the last twelve months, there'd been a few additions. His nephew. Christopher and his two children. Josh.

He was thrilled for Shelby and Josh, but it seemed to highlight his solitude even more. He glanced down at his eggnog. Maybe he should have something stronger. While he was excited for his cousin and her husband, their joy made his melancholy more acute.

The song on the sound system changed to a rocking Christmas favorite, and Jack glanced at the Christmas tree in the living room. It wasn't the additions that had him feeling out of sorts. It was the absences— of one woman in particular. He'd thought about driving to Mel's Books and convincing her to join him for the party, but he couldn't.

Wouldn't.

She was probably off with Marius, meeting his mother and finally being a part of a family Christmas with the man she loved like she'd always wanted to be.

Shelby sidled up to him and looked him over. "Mr. and Mrs. Henderson standing by the tree mentioned they saw you and Stacey out for dinner. What's going on there? Are you two trying to get back together?"

He grimaced. "Didn't work out."

"That sure didn't take long. What happened?"

"It was over before it really got started. I don't know what I was thinking."

"You were thinking that she's not Melanie. And you're right. Stacey could never hold a candle to Mel."

"I guess it's true that you can never go home again." He took a gulp of his eggnog, spotting Aunt Sarah and Mr. Duffy sitting on the sofa. He waved and turned back to his cousin. "Let me wallow in my misery, okay? That's what the holidays are for after all."

Shelby rolled her eyes at him. "So what did you find out in the testing of your theory about relationships?"

"That it's not my job that got in between me and my girlfriends." He stared into his almost empty cup and realized what he should have realized years ago. "It was never really about all the time I spent at work."

"No, it wasn't." She peered at him. "It was Mel all along."

He gave a short nod. "And now that I know that, she's moved on."

Shelby opened her mouth, but whatever she was going to say was interrupted by Uncle Mark giving a holler as he opened a gift, then crushing Penny into a hug. Shelby frowned. "Wonder what that's all about."

Uncle Mark wiped his eyes, then turned to the others who watched him. He unfolded the T-shirt he'd unwrapped. It said "Papa" and a date the following summer. "Penny and Christopher are making me a grandpa this June!"

Everyone clapped and cheered, and the parents-to-be were toasted.

Shelby smiled and leaned in closer to Jack. "We're due a month apart. She told me earlier tonight."

Jack looked at her. "You're..."

Shelby nodded, a knowing smile on her

face. "Yes, but we're not telling everyone just yet. So keep it under wraps."

Jack made a zipping motion in front of his mouth, then drained the rest of his eggnog. "Think I'll go talk to Aunt Sarah. She mentioned that she had something to say to me earlier."

He moved off in the direction of his great-aunt and her fiancé. Aunt Sarah pointed to the empty spot on the sofa next to her. "Take a seat, Jack."

He did, waiting and hoping for the request to come. Aunt Sarah didn't disappoint. She glanced at Mr. Duffy briefly, before saying, "Jack, I would love it if you would walk me down the aisle on New Year's Day."

Jack grinned. "Of course. I'm honored. But are you sure I should be the one? Uncle Mark is the oldest guy in the family."

"But you've always been my favorite great-nephew."

He let out a laugh. "I'm your only great-nephew."

"And that makes you special."

She smiled and patted one of his cheeks, then left him sitting next to Mr. Duffy, muttering something about getting more hors d'oeuvres. Mr. Duffy scooted closer to Jack in her absence. "Sarah thought I should also talk to you alone. Man to man."

"Sure. What's on your mind?"

"I look at you, and I see a lot of myself. You have a lot of good qualities, and I think maybe too much pride to admit to that friend of yours that you were wrong about your feelings for her."

"Now wait a minute. I tried to tell her."

"But did you make yourself vulnerable to her to the point that you showed her your heart?"

Jack would never have predicted that one day he'd be getting relationship advice from Mr. Duffy who his aunt had once referred to as Mr. Grumpy. But the man had a point. Jack hadn't really explained himself well the night he'd kissed Mel. If he had, she might be here with him instead of off somewhere with her new boyfriend.

"You know the story about me and your aunt, right?"

The story had recently come to light in the Cuthbert family. Mr. Duffy and Aunt Sarah had gotten engaged before the Korean War started, but he didn't want to marry until he came home safe and sound first. When he did come home, eventually, he was injured, bitter, and it drove a wedge between them. He left Sarah waiting at the altar. Years of resentment and hurt feelings kept them apart.

"It wasn't until I realized I should have trusted in Sarah, in us, all those years ago, and admitted to her that I had been wrong. That I wanted a second chance at love with her. Only then could we move on from the past."

"And now you're starting your future, getting married next week."

Mr. Duffy peered at him. "Do you understand what I'm saying?"

"That I need to admit I was wrong and ask for another shot with Melanie?"

"And it wouldn't hurt to grovel a little. To be with a woman that loving and beautiful, it would be worth it." Mr. Duffy motioned to the Christmas tree.

Jack turned to find Melanie standing by the tree, a gift in her hands. She smiled when she saw him and motioned him over. Jack thanked Mr. Duffy. "Good luck, son."

Jack went to a beaming Mel. "I didn't think you would be coming to the party tonight." He glanced behind her, thinking that Marius would appear. But there was no sign of the guy. "Are you here alone?"

Mel shrugged. "Yes, nothing could keep me away from the Cuthbert Christmas Eve party. We always said that we would be each other's date at Christmas if we were both single."

Jack nodded, remembering the pact they'd made when they were in high school, then paused. If they were both single… "I ended things with Stacey."

Mel nodded. "I know. Shelby told me."

"But what about—"

She thrust the brightly wrapped package she was holding into his hands before he could ask about Marius. "Here. Open this."

Jack looked at the present. "I'm sorry, I didn't bring your gift with me."

She waved off the words. "I'll get it later. Now open it."

He quickly unwrapped the package. He was shocked to see the book was by one of his favorite authors. "This isn't supposed to be out for months."

"A friend of a friend is her agent, so I called in a favor to get an early copy. Open the cover."

He did so and found a personalized message signed from the author. His jaw dropped. "Mel…" He clutched the book to his chest. "I can't tell you how much this means to me."

She reached up and kissed his cheek. "Merry Christmas."

He should tell her. He should do what Mr. Duffy had advised. He should grovel and tell her he had been wrong. Instead, he repeated her words back to her. "Merry Christmas."

ONCE THE CAROLS had been sung and the children had each opened a gift, the partygoers started to dwindle. Melanie always watched the parents bundle up their kids and carry them out to the car with a little twinge of jealousy. Shaking her head, she reminded herself that she was done with what-ifs. Better to focus on the here and now instead of a dreamed-up future. Jack handed her another cup of eggnog and nudged her shoulder. "What are you thinking about?"

She sighed. "I thought that getting a makeover would turn out to be like it is in the fairy tales. That a magic wand would be waved over my life and poof. Happy ever after."

"But we don't live in a fairy-tale world."

"Don't get me wrong. There have been some good things to come out of this. I feel more confident about myself. And that has spilled into all aspects of my life. I'm grateful for that."

"And your relationship with your dad has gotten better."

"Exactly."

"And you have Marius."

She bit her lip, realizing no one had told him the news. "We're not together anymore."

Was that hope she read on Jack's face? She reminded herself to keep her focus on their friendship. "One major thing I've realized these past months is that you were right."

He frowned at her words. "What was I so right about?"

"Our friendship is too important to risk. And I was wrong for trying to make it into something it couldn't be."

"Mel…"

"Hey, you two. Look where you are!" Shelby pointed to the mistletoe hanging above them.

Mel glanced up and groaned. "I thought Aunt Sarah was the one who always put up the mistletoe."

"Maybe Penny and Christopher are keeping up her tradition." He looked at her and gave a one-shouldered shrug. "What do you say? It is tradition after all."

"Well, in the spirit of Christmas then."

"And our friendship."

"Of course. Our friendship always."

She closed her eyes and Jack gently put his hands on her shoulders. She'd meant it to be a quick peck, but once their lips touched, the kiss seemed to take over.

She wasn't complaining and neither was Jack.

When the kiss finally ended and she opened her eyes, she saw Jack smiling, but a more serious look she couldn't name flashed in his eyes. The magic of the moment had passed. "I'm glad you showed up tonight," he told her.

"Me too."

She didn't want to believe that would be their last kiss.

MEL EMERGED FROM her bubble bath and wrapped herself inside the new plush velour robe that she'd purchased as a Christmas gift to herself. She had big plans with a bottle of wine and watching her favorite Christmas movie. Once she had changed into a new pair of flannel pajamas, she settled on the couch and poured the first glass of wine before pressing Play on the remote control. Dickens curled up beside her on the sofa as the movie began.

Turning her head from the television screen, she noted that it had started to snow outside. Maybe it would be a white Christmas after all. She paused the movie and walked to the front window to stare out at the small flakes that floated down and settled on her front lawn. Smiling, she returned to the couch and turned off all the lights except for the Christmas tree and resumed her movie.

Little Mary had promised George she'd love him until the day she died, and Mel knew that it was the same with her for Jack. He could stay her best friend with no romantic ties, but she'd still love him. Pine for him. Ache for him.

Her cell phone buzzed. A text from her dad. Merry Christmas, punkin.

He had used a nickname he hadn't used in years. Maybe she wasn't the only one feeling sentimental that evening. She typed a quick reply, Merry Christmas to you and Betty. With love.

Try as she might, she couldn't fault her father for not being able to be there for her like she wanted. He had been capable of only what he'd been capable of back then. And no amount of wishing things were different on her part would change that fact.

And, she realized, Jack was the same now.

She turned back to her movie and pulled the quilt up to her chin. Her phone buzzed again. What are you doing? Shelby was checking up on her. Kind but not necessary.

Watching my favorite Christmas movie and drinking wine. How was your first Christmas with your husband?

Wonderful. Amazing. And to think next year we'll add to our family.

No more texts, so Mel returned to her movie until her phone buzzed again.

Are you okay being alone today?

I'm fine. And she was. On Halloween, she had vowed that she'd never spend another holiday alone, yet here she was. Alone again. And she discovered that she was okay with that. The only person she could count on was herself.

The longer the movie played and the more of the wine Mel drank, the more she sank into the sofa. The holidays made her miss her mother even more. She could certainly use her advice about what to do next. Her father had never moved on from her mother, and Mel couldn't seem to give up the hope of Jack. Maybe it was a Beach trait. When they loved, it was for life.

The movie ended, and Mel turned off the television and lay on the couch, staring at the lights on the Christmas tree. There was something comforting about their glow that lulled her into a peace and calmness.

Her cell phone ringing brought her head up. Jack's face lit up her screen. She smiled as she answered, "Merry Christmas, Jack. How was your family dinner?"

"Good. Some year I'm going to convince you to come with me."

She grinned at the thought. "Maybe next year."

"How was your favorite movie?"

"Love and friendship triumphed in the end like always." He knew her so well. Knew she'd read until it got dark out, then put in her favorite movie. She reached over and stroked Dickens's head. "It was nice to share it with the new man in my life. Dickens says hello by the way."

"You're happy with him?"

"You were right about him too. I should have gotten a dog a long time ago. I never realized how comforting it is to have him around."

"I'm not always right."

"In my mind, you are."

Jack stayed silent on the other end. "Shelby mentioned that Josh is having a New Year's Eve party at the community center. Like a preinauguration party. Are you going?"

Mel had considered turning down the invitation when Shelby had extended it to her the night before. Arriving alone to a party on New Year's Eve was always a tough one for a single person. Almost as bad as facing Valentine's Day as a party of one. "I don't know."

"Do you have other plans?"

"No. Are you going?" Maybe if she could go with Jack, it wouldn't be so bad. "The clinic closes at six, and the party starts at eight so that gives you plenty of time to go home and change."

"I'm on call until eleven or so when the overnight tech comes in."

"Oh. Well, maybe you could come after."

"I don't know."

"At least promise you'll try to make it before midnight."

"For you. I'll try."

CHAPTER TWELVE

MEL PICKED UP a piece of Gouda cheese from the charcuterie board and nibbled on it as she surveyed the people gathered at the community center. Most of them were couples with a few single Cuthbert cousins and friends thrown into the mix. Shelby approached her with a glass of white wine and handed it to her.

"Promise me that you won't end our friendship."

Mel took a sip of the wine. "That's an interesting way to start a conversation."

"Josh has a friend that he thinks you should meet." Shelby glanced over her shoulder to where her husband stood talking to a man wearing a cardboard hat with "Happy New Year" written in glitter on his head.

Mel pursed her lips, trying not to laugh.

"You set me up on a date for New Year's Eve? Really?"

"I know what you said about no more setups, but it doesn't hurt to at least meet him."

"It seems pointless, but sure."

Shelby turned back to her and leaned in closer. "All right, he's coming over here. Be nice."

"I'm always nice."

Mel took another sip of her drink before looking the guy over. He was cute, especially with the silly hat on top of his head. He'd dressed more formally than most of the other party guests in a shirt and tie with khakis, but it gave him an intriguing nerdy quality that she'd been known to be drawn to in the past. She smiled when Josh introduced him as Vic who served as Thora's city attorney. Mel stuck out her hand. He had a firm handshake and an easy smile. "Nice to meet you, Vic. Tell me. Are you a reader?"

Vic looked worried. "I used to be, but I haven't found much time to read for pleasure lately."

She nodded. "That happens to a lot of people. What did you used to read?"

"I like fantasies. You ever hear of Tyler Meesto's trilogy?"

She'd been ordering extra copies of the series for months since she couldn't seem to keep her shelves stocked with them. "*The Elves of Simario Chronicles*? Of course. You know, he's coming out with the first book of a new series in March."

Shelby patted her arm before moving to the other side of the room with Josh who beamed as if he'd won some kind of bet.

"I hadn't heard that. So you're into fantasy novels too?"

"Not so much, but I'm into books. Josh might have mentioned it, but I own the bookstore downtown, so I try to keep track of what's happening in the publishing world. And I tend to read a lot of different genres."

Vic stopped nibbling on the crudités on his plastic plate and sighed. "Man, I'd love to own a bookstore. That was my dream as a kid. To do that or spend the night in the library."

She knew the feeling since she'd felt the

same way. "If you love books so much, why aren't you reading more?"

They chatted for a while about his job as a lawyer which used up a lot of his time, especially since he took on quite a few pro bono cases in what spare time he had. She watched him as he talked. He was a nice guy. And maybe if she'd met him at the beginning of her dating search, she might have been interested. But if Marius couldn't get her over Jack, then Vic likely wouldn't either.

She listened to his stories and answered him politely, but her mind wasn't focused on the conversation. Instead, she wondered where Jack was tonight. Shelby had said he had plans after he left the clinic, but hadn't expanded on what they were. Was he on a date with someone new? And would he kiss his date at midnight? And why should she care if he did or not?

She realized that Vic had asked her something. "I'm sorry. What was the question?"

"I asked if you'd be interested in getting together for drinks sometime. Maybe talk more about books. Tyler Meesto's newest, for example."

She looked into his hazel-green eyes and regretted that despite his interest in her, she couldn't show the same to him. "Vic, you seem like a really nice guy. And if things were different with me, I would take you up on that offer."

"But there's someone else?"

She nodded slowly. There would always be someone else. Like her father, she felt there was only one love of her life. It would always be Jack. "I'm sorry."

"Well, if things don't work out with him, I hope you'll look me up." He reached into his pocket and pulled out a business card from his wallet, handing it to her. "I like a woman who is interested in books."

She pocketed the card. "I will keep that in mind. And stop by my store sometime. I think you need to make a New Year's resolution to read more for pleasure."

"I will." Vic looked around the room. "I think I'll go and try the bacon dip. Josh said it was amazing."

He left her, and Shelby took the space

he had once occupied. "That was quick. What was wrong with him?"

Mel looked at her friend. "He'll never be Jack." She handed Shelby her half-full glass of wine. "Thank you for inviting me tonight, but I think I need to go home and do some thinking. I'm not much in a party mood."

"But it's not even midnight. You can't leave before then. Don't go, Mel."

Mel kissed her on the cheek. "I'll see you guys tomorrow morning at Josh's inauguration ceremony at City Hall."

Before Shelby could talk her out of it, Mel left the party and drove home. She passed several other house parties. A few packed parking lots at bars and restaurants. Even her neighbor had a few people over, but she wasn't interested in spending the evening in the midst of a crowd. No, she wanted to be alone. To consider the past year and make a plan for the next.

So maybe she wouldn't have anyone if she couldn't have Jack. And she was okay with that. They'd always be friends.

Best friends to the end.

She would be just fine on her own.

Once home, she changed into comfy sweatpants and a loose sweatshirt before settling on her sofa with her journal and a gel pen. She wanted to get all of her thoughts onto paper. Say goodbye to one year before welcoming the next.

THE GERMAN SHEPHERD puppies scrambled to get to the food. Jack even had to separate two who yipped at each other. "There's plenty here for all of you. You need to learn to take your turn."

He sat on the floor next to them and pondered his life since a new year was about to start and provide him with three hundred and sixty-five more opportunities to make a change for the better. Because he didn't think he could keep doing what he always had been and find a different outcome.

Missed chances for the past year brought Mel's face to mind. He'd been unsure of what to say to her when he'd called her on Christmas Day. The holiday hadn't been the same even though he had spent the time with his family and without her like always. He'd gotten nice gifts, but the books he'd received from his parents only reminded him of Mel. In fact, everything had made him think of her. The meal had featured prime rib which he knew was one of her favorites. His sister had made a blueberry torte that he knew Mel would love. Even holding his nephew, Gavin, and playing with a stuffed toy only reminded him of the movie he'd watched with Mel that featured the same character.

He missed her. Wanted to be with her.

He should have told her that he loved her before that kiss under the mistletoe. After the kiss even. That he'd been wrong, like Mr. Duffy had told him. But he'd let the moment go. Then she'd gone and told him he'd been right all along about not risking their friendship.

Only he'd been wrong. So wrong.

He sighed and moved one of the puppies to a free spot at the food bowl rather than have her climb over another to get to it.

He'd been tempted to go to the party at the community center when Alison came in for her shift at eleven, but he didn't think he could play it cool on a just-friends level with Mel. Not on tonight of all nights. Because as he looked back on the past year, he realized there was a hole that only she could fill.

She was his best friend. His partner. The love of his life.

And the thought of looking at a New Year without her only made that hole feel even bigger. No, it was better that he skip the party and take care of things here at the clinic since he'd be tied up the entire following day with attending Josh's inauguration, then giving the bride away at Aunt Sarah's wedding.

Mel would be there for both. Jack knew he'd have to pretend that friendship could be enough for him.

It had to be enough. Because he couldn't accept anything less. Friends to the end. That would be him and Mel. And if she eventually married someone else...

He groaned and bent forward at the waist. One of the pups approached him and started to lick his face. He held the puppy and snuggled him close to his chest. "Thanks, buddy. But I think my heart needs more than a kiss from you."

It needed a kiss from Mel. For some reason that he couldn't name, he still had hope. He had to give their relationship one more chance before giving up on it forever. And what better time than New Year's Eve?

He set the puppy down and raced out of the clinic. Driving to the community center, he cursed the red lights that seemed to impede his progress. She was and would always be the love of his life. It had taken him too long to realize it. This wasn't a passing attraction or a moment of madness. This was love with a capital *L*. True Love. Lasting Love. Forever Love.

He arrived at the center of town and had barely put the car into Park before he was sprinting up to the double doors. Josh approached him just as he entered the community center and was surveying the large room. "Jack, you almost missed the big moment. We're getting close to midnight."

"Mel. Where is she?"

Shelby appeared behind Josh. "She's not here. She left a while ago."

"Why would she leave before midnight?"

Shelby sighed and shook her head. "She

wanted to be alone. Probably wanted to do some thinking."

"She even turned down my friend, who asked her out," Josh said.

Shelby patted his arm. "Let it go, love."

Jack couldn't keep the smile off his face. "That means I might still have a chance with her."

"If the two of you are going to make a relationship work, you need to learn how to communicate better."

"Fine. We'll do that next year." He leaned forward and kissed Shelby on the cheek and vigorously shook Josh's hand, before turning and running back to his car.

"Where are you going?" Shelby shouted.

"To kiss Mel before it's midnight." He gave a quick wave, then jumped into his car. If Mel had left early, she was in one of two places: at the bookstore or at home. He'd bet that she'd gone home. He put his car into gear and zoomed out of the parking lot. Only eleven minutes left until midnight. He had to get to Mel quick.

MEL OPENED HER eyes and rubbed them. She must have drifted off because she couldn't remember falling sleep, but a glance at the clock told her it was almost a new year. She rose to her feet and straightened the living room before walking down the hall to her bedroom. Her mind might want her to stay up and welcome the New Year, but her body was obviously telling her that she needed some sleep.

Her heart on the other hand searched for peace.

Despite writing down her thoughts in her journal and looking to the future, she felt more restless than before. As if she was anticipating something big to come and change her life. All she needed to do was to be open and available when the opportunity arose.

A pounding on her front door. Dickens started barking before springing off the bed and racing away to investigate. Groaning, she put her bathrobe back on and walked down the darkened hallway to peer out the peephole of her front door. What was Jack doing here?

She opened the door, and Jack peered behind her. "We need to talk."

"Um, don't we talk enough?"

"Not about the stuff that really matters." He quickly came inside and shut the door behind him. "Because here's the thing. What I really need to tell you. And it's that I love you."

When she started to say something, he put his finger on her lips, his eyes on them. "No, please, I need to say this." He inhaled a deep breath, then took her hands in his. "You said that I was only attracted to you because someone else wanted you. As if you were a toy that I only wanted because someone else was playing with you. But that's wrong. I've never thought of you as someone to play with. You're far too precious, worth so much more than to do that."

She looked at him, at their hands entwined. What was he saying? Did he really mean what she thought he did? She looked back up at him and searched his face. "You said you love me."

"I do. And I'm not talking about friendship, but the kind of love that lasts a lifetime. I mean, the kind of love that makes me ache when you're not around. The kind that makes my heart speed up when I see that you sent me a text. It's a love that I didn't recognize because it started when we were five years old. I'll admit that I took it for granted for so many years, but I came here tonight to tell you that I love you. That I'm in love with you. And I can't spend another single minute without you."

Mel's heart had stopped the moment she'd seen Jack standing there, but it started to beat again in tempo with his words. She pulled him forward, drawing him inside the house and shutting the door behind him. "I don't want to be without you either."

He put his hands on her waist and drew her to him. "Not ever."

"Never."

He started to lean forward, but she backed away. "We need to agree on a few things before I'll let you kiss me."

Jack smiled. "Oooo-kaaaay…"

"If this is going to work out between us, then I need to be able to be completely honest with you about my feelings."

"Agreed."

"And to be absolutely truthful start-ing now, I want forever with you. I want the big wedding. I want a house that we pick out together. And it's got to be large enough for a family. I'm thinking at least two kids because I won't have our children be lonely."

"How about three?"

She smiled back. "Fine. We'll compromise at four."

He laughed. "And I'm going to want an extended backyard at that house for the two dogs." Dickens woofed as if agreeing too.

"Two dogs?"

"We could compromise at four. And a cat or three."

She held up a hand. "Okay, two dogs. Three cats. Four kids."

"And lots of love."

"I can kiss to that."

He dipped his head and kissed her. The best kiss ever, filled with love and longing and a sweetness she reveled in.

A loud bang outside drew them apart. She smiled. "Fireworks for us?"

Jack beamed at her. "Every time we kiss."

She laughed and nodded. He kissed her

once more, then rested his forehead against hers. "I should go. Tomorrow will be a long day."

"A long day, but one full of celebrations."

"Of love too." He put a hand on her cheek. "I love you, Mel."

"I love you too." Mel closed her eyes. "I'll be counting down the minutes until I see you again. Happy New Year, Jack."

"Happy new life, my love."

THE WEDDING VOWS had been exchanged by the older couple, and as Sarah and Henry took their first kiss as husband and wife there were more than a few joyful tears shed. Happiness radiated off them as the minister presented the newly married couple to the crowd.

Jack took his role as the one who had given Aunt Sarah away seriously. And as such, he stepped forward and welcomed Henry to the family before turning to his great-aunt and kissing both of her cheeks. "I hope that the two of you always stay as happy as you are today."

She glanced over his shoulder to where

Mel sat in the second row of the church, beaming at them. "I wish the same for you, my dear boy."

Jack turned and exchanged a smile with Mel. "I intend to be as happy as you very, very soon."

She laughed and raised her bouquet in victory. "I knew it. The moment I saw you at the inauguration today, I knew that you had finally come to your senses and realized what the rest of us have known for years. Congratulations, Jack. You deserve to love and be loved."

He hugged her tightly, then stepped away so other family members could get their turn wishing the newlyweds love and happiness. He went and stood next to Mel who still dabbed at her eyes with a tissue. "Why are you crying?"

"I always cry at weddings. And this one was extra special." She put an arm around his waist and stared into his eyes. "Do you think we'll still be in love when we're their age?"

"I intend to be." He pulled her close and kissed the top of her head.

The reception was held in the same ballroom where the fundraiser had been held only a few weeks before. As Jack pulled out Mel's chair for her at a table decorated with white roses and candlelight, he marveled at how much had changed in such a short time. To be honest, a lot of things had changed for himself and his family within the past year. They'd lost elections, jobs and barriers to love which gained them husbands, babies, job opportunities and new directions.

He turned to Mel who reached over and took his hand. And soon, he'd gain a wife, he hoped. She was already married to him in his heart, but he wanted to make it official and public. He leaned over to her. "What do you think about a spring wedding? Maybe in April?"

Her mouth dropped open. "This April? As in only a few months away? Are you serious?"

"I don't want to wait any longer than necessary, do you?"

Mel called out to Shelby, "He wants us to get married this spring."

Shelby stared at him. "Do you realize

how much time it takes to get a wedding planned? We need months and months."

"You and Josh seemed to get married all right, and it only took hours after you proposed to him."

Shelby turned to look at her husband who stood talking to Christopher. "That's fair. When you know what you want, it doesn't require a lot of time or planning."

Jack smiled at Mel. "Well, I know what I want. And she's sitting right here next to me."

Mel returned the smile. "I always wished you'd use those romantic words on me."

"*All* my mushy words are exclusively for you from now on. That's a promise."

Penny took a seat at the table and sighed, putting her feet up on an empty chair. "I can't wait to get out of these dress shoes. Give me a turnout and steel-toed boots any day." She looked over at Mel. "So did he finally confess his love to you?"

"Last night," Mel said and blushed. "Right around midnight."

"It's been quite a year for us, hasn't it?"

Jack nodded. "I was thinking the same

thing earlier. We've lost some, but we've gained so much more."

"I think we needed to lose in order to find out what was important to us," Shelby said. Again, she glanced at Josh. "If I hadn't lost the election, I don't know that I'd be so happy. And if you had told me that months ago, I would have laughed or argued with you."

"If Christopher hadn't lost his house, would I have ever met him? He lived only a few doors down from Aunt Sarah, but I never noticed him before that day." Penny's loving expression directed at Christopher said it all really.

Mel turned to Jack. "And what did you have to lose?"

"Fear. Insecurity. And I had to lose you for a time to finally see what I wanted was right in front of me all these years."

Shelby nodded and raised her water glass. "Well said."

Josh and Christopher joined them. "Why is everyone looking so serious? I thought that we were here to celebrate," Josh said, then held out his hand to Shelby. "I, for one, intend on dancing the evening away with my beautiful wife."

Christopher nodded. "Sounds like a good plan. Pen?"

She groaned, but smiled as he helped her to her feet and led her to the dance floor. Jack reached over and gave a Mel a quick peck. "Let's show them what real dancing looks like."

AT THE HEAD TABLE, Great-aunt Sarah watched the three couples dancing. She'd brought that about through her matchmaking. She was grateful it had paid off, and so handsomely. And speaking of handsome, to her new husband, she said, "Love is all that matters in the end, isn't it?"

He grasped her hand in his and kissed it. "Love always wins."

* * * * *

If you missed Penny and Christopher's romance, or Shelby and Josh's, visit www.Harlequin.com today for A Hero for the Holidays *and* The Bad Boy's Redemption*!*

Get 4 FREE REWARDS!

We'll send you 2 FREE Books plus 2 FREE Mystery Gifts.

Love Inspired books feature uplifting stories where faith helps guide you through life's challenges and discover the promise of a new beginning.

FREE Value Over $20

YES! Please send me 2 FREE Love Inspired Romance novels and my 2 FREE mystery gifts (gifts are worth about $10 retail). After receiving them, if I don't wish to receive any more books, I can return the shipping statement marked "cancel." If I don't cancel, I will receive 6 brand-new novels every month and be billed just $5.24 each for the regular-print edition or $5.99 each for the larger-print edition in the U.S., or $5.74 each for the regular-print edition or $6.24 each for the larger-print edition in Canada. That's a savings of at least 13% off the cover price. It's quite a bargain! Shipping and handling is just 50¢ per book in the U.S. and $1.25 per book in Canada.* I understand that accepting the 2 free books and gifts places me under no obligation to buy anything. I can always return a shipment and cancel at any time. The free books and gifts are mine to keep no matter what I decide.

Choose one: ☐ **Love Inspired Romance Regular-Print** (105/305 IDN GNWC)   ☐ **Love Inspired Romance Larger-Print** (122/322 IDN GNWC)

Name (please print)

Address   Apt. #

City   State/Province   Zip/Postal Code

Email: Please check this box ☐ if you would like to receive newsletters and promotional emails from Harlequin Enterprises ULC and its affiliates. You can unsubscribe anytime.

> Mail to the **Harlequin Reader Service:**
> **IN U.S.A.:** P.O. Box 1341, Buffalo, NY 14240-8531
> **IN CANADA:** P.O. Box 603, Fort Erie, Ontario L2A 5X3

Want to try 2 free books from another series! Call 1-800-873-8635 or visit www.ReaderService.com.

---

*Terms and prices subject to change without notice. Prices do not include sales taxes, which will be charged (if applicable) based on your state or country of residence. Canadian residents will be charged applicable taxes. Offer not valid in Quebec. This offer is limited to one order per household. Books received may not be as shown. Not valid for current subscribers to Love Inspired Romance books. All orders subject to approval. Credit or debit balances in a customer's account(s) may be offset by any other outstanding balance owed by or to the customer. Please allow 4 to 6 weeks for delivery. Offer available while quantities last.

Your Privacy—Your information is being collected by Harlequin Enterprises ULC, operating as Harlequin Reader Service. For a complete summary of the information we collect, how we use this information and to whom it is disclosed, please visit our privacy notice located at corporate.harlequin.com/privacy-notice. From time to time we may also exchange your personal information with reputable third parties. If you wish to opt out of this sharing of your personal information, please visit readerservice.com/consumerschoice or call 1-800-873-8635. **Notice to California Residents**—Under California law, you have specific rights to control and access your data. For more information on these rights and how to exercise them, visit corporate.harlequin.com/california-privacy.

LIR21R2

HARLEQUIN SELECTS COLLECTION

19 FREE BOOKS IN ALL!

From Robyn Carr to RaeAnne Thayne to Linda Lael Miller and Sherryl Woods we promise (actually, GUARANTEE!) each author in the Harlequin Selects collection has seen their name on the *New York Times* or *USA TODAY* bestseller lists!

YES! Please send me the **Harlequin Selects Collection**. This collection begins with 3 FREE books and 2 FREE gifts in the first shipment. Along with my 3 free books, I'll also get 4 more books from the Harlequin Selects Collection, which I may either return and owe nothing or keep for the low price of $24.14 U.S./$28.82 CAN. each plus $2.99 U.S./$7.49 CAN. for shipping and handling per shipment*.If I decide to continue, I will get 6 or 7 more books (about once a month for 7 months) but will only need to pay for 4. That means 2 or 3 books in every shipment will be FREE! If I decide to keep the entire collection, I'll have paid for only 32 books because 19 were FREE! I understand that accepting the 3 free books and gifts places me under no obligation to buy anything. I can always return a shipment and cancel at any time. My free books and gifts are mine to keep no matter what I decide.

☐ 262 HCN 5576   ☐ 462 HCN 5576

Name (please print)

Address   Apt. #

City   State/Province   Zip/Postal Code

Mail to the **Harlequin Reader Service:**
IN U.S.A.: P.O. Box 1341, Buffalo, NY 14240-8531
IN CANADA: P.O. Box 603, Fort Erie, Ontario L2A 5X3

Get 4 FREE REWARDS!

We'll send you 2 FREE Books plus 2 FREE Mystery Gifts.

FREE Value Over **$20**

Both the **Romance** and **Suspense** collections feature compelling novels written by many of today's bestselling authors.